THE MAGIC
OF AVALON . . .

The fox sat on his haunches and reared up, holding his front paws in the air. For some reason, Sara sat down, her hands on the ground as if she must copy the usual four-footed position of the fox.

Thin trails of mist rose from the leaf piles. The smoke grew thicker, and she could not see anything.

She wondered if she were dreaming all this, for everything looked so odd; and, frightened, she tried to get up. But her hands did not push properly—in fact, she no longer had hands!

Paws covered with gray fur rested on the ground. And there was the same gray fur up her arms! Gray fur all over her body— a gray tail behind her.

Sara tried to scream, but the sound she made was very different—"Merrow!" That was the wail of a terrified cat!

Who—what was she? And how did she get that way?

Andre Norton

Steel Magic

Illustrated by Robin Jacques

AN ARCHWAY PAPERBACK
POCKET BOOKS • NEW YORK

POCKET BOOKS, a Simon & Schuster division of
GULF & WESTERN CORPORATION
1230 Avenue of the Americas, New York, N.Y. 10020

Copyright © 1965 by Andre Norton

Illustrations © 1967 by Robin Jacques

ISBN: 0-671-29901-8

First Pocket Books printing August, 1978

1 2 9 8

Trademarks registered in the United States and other countries.

Printed in the U.S.A.

For Stephen, Greg, Eric, Peter,
Donald, Alexander, and Jeffrey.
And for Kristen and Deborah,
who love stories of fairy worlds.

Contents

The Lake
and the Castle

The adventure began with the picnic basket that Sara Lowry won at the Firemen's Strawberry Festival at Ternsport Village. Because it was the first time any of the junior Lowrys had ever won anything, they could hardly believe it when Chief Loomis called out the number of the ticket Sara had knotted into one corner of her handkerchief. Both Greg and Eric had to hustle her up to the platform where Chief Loomis waited beside the loud-speaker.

The basket was super, the boys agreed as soon as they had a chance to examine it. Inside the lid, fastened in a piece of webbing, were forks, spoons, and knives of stainless steel, and there was a set of four cups—blue, yellow, green, and fire-engine red—with matching plastic plates. Sara was still

1

so surprised at her luck that she would not have been astonished if the basket had vanished completely before she carried it back to Uncle Mac's station wagon.

When Uncle Mac slowed down for the sharp turn into the Tern Manor private road, Sara clutched the basket handles tighter. Greg's sharp elbow dug into her ribs, but she did not try to wriggle away. This place was spooky at night, and she did not wonder that Greg moved back from the window when ragged branches reached out as if they were trying to drag the car off the narrow road into all those shadows. At night you had to keep thinking about how this was still New York State, with the Hudson River only two hills and three fields away—and not a scary country out of a fairy tale.

Now they were passing the dark place where the big house had once stood. Twenty years ago it had burned down, long before Uncle Mac had bought the old carriage house and the ground with the gardens for what he called his hideaway. Uncle Mac wrote books and wanted peace and quiet when he was working—lots of it. But the old cellar holes still marked where the house had stood, and the Lowrys had been strictly warned not to explore there. Since Uncle Mac was perfectly reasonable about letting them go everywhere else through the overgrown gardens and the little piece of woodland, the Lowrys were content.

They drove into the old stable yard. When the big house had been built fifty years ago, there had been horses here, and people had actually ridden in the funny carriage the children had found crowded into part of an old barn. But now the station wagon occupied the main part of the barn and there were no horses.

Mrs. Steiner, the housekeeper, was waiting on the doorstep of the carriage house and she waved an air mail–special delivery letter at Uncle Mac the minute he got out of the car. She was also wearing one of her own special "past-your-bed-time-and-hurry-in-before-I-miss-my-favorite-TV-program" looks for the Lowrys. Mrs. Steiner spoke with authority, whereas Uncle Mac, especially while writing, would sometimes absent-mindedly agree to interesting changes of rules and regulations. Uncle Mac was not used to children. Mrs. Steiner was, and an opponent to be respected in any tug of wills.

On the whole the Lowry children had been looking forward to a good summer. In spite of Mrs. Steiner there were advantages to staying at Tern Manor. Since Dad had been ordered to Japan on special service and had taken Mother with him for two months, Uncle Mac's was far better than just second best.

When one was used to towns and not the counry, though, what was left of the old estate could be frightening at times. Greg had gone to scout camp, and Eric had taken overnight hikes

3

in the state park when Dad was stationed at the big air base in Colorado. But this was Sara's first visit to a piece of the outdoors that had been allowed to run wild, just as it pleased. She was still afraid of so many big, shaggy bushes and tall trees, and managed to have one of the boys with her whenever she went too far from the stable yard or the road.

Mrs. Steiner spoke darkly of snakes, but they did not frighten Sara. Pictures of snakes in library books were interesting, and to watch one going about its business might be fun. But poison ivy and "those nasty bugs," which Mrs. Steiner also mentioned at length, were another matter. Sara did not like to think about bugs, especially the kind that had a large number of legs and might investigate humans. Spiders were far more unpleasant than snakes, she had long ago decided. She was really afraid of them, though she knew that was silly. But to see one scurrying along on all those legs—ugh! As they climbed the stairs to the small bedrooms in the top story of the carriage house, Eric joggled the basket Sara still carried.

"Let's fill this up tomorrow and really go exploring—for the whole day!"

"Might be a good time to hunt for the lake," Greg agreed. "We'll ask Uncle Mac at breakfast —after he's had his third cup of coffee."

"Mrs. Steiner say there's liable to be snakes there," Sara offered. Please, she added to herself, just no *big* spiders, little ones were bad enough. Greg snorted and Eric stamped hard on the next step. "Mrs. Steiner sees snakes everywhere, when she isn't seeing something else as bad. Water snakes, maybe, and I'd like to get me one of those for a pet. Anyway, we've wanted to find the lake ever since Uncle Mac told us there was one."

This was perfectly true. The legend of the lost lake as Uncle Mac had told it was enough to excite all three Lowrys. The gardens were now a matted jungle, but they had been planned to encircle an ornamental lake. Mr. Brosius had bought the land more than fifty years ago, throwing three riverside farms together and spending a great deal of time and money developing the estate. He was a legend, too, was Mr. Brosius, a stranger with a long beard, who had paid for all the costs of the manor's building in gold coins. Then he had gone and the house had burned.

Nobody had been quite sure who really owned the manor, and finally it had been sold for taxes. Farmers had bought the fields, and the part with the gardens had gone to a real-estate man who finally sold it to Uncle Mac. And Uncle Mac had never cared enough to plow through all the brambles and brush to see if there was a lake any more. In fact he said he was sure it must have dried up a long time ago.

Sara wondered if that was true. She paused in her undressing to open the picnic basket and gloat over its contents just once more. What if Uncle

Mac had not taken them to the festival tonight, or if she had not had her allowance in her purse and could not have bought that dime ticket? Maybe if she had not won the basket the boys would not have included her in the lake hunt. This was going to be a fine summer!

After she had turned off the light, she sat up in bed. This was the first night she had not stood by the window listening to all the queer little sounds which were a part of the night outside. It was so easy to believe that there were things out there which were never to be sighted by day, things as lost as the lake and maybe even stranger. . . .

But tonight she thought instead of packing the picnic basket. And with plans of peanut-butter sandwiches and hard-boiled eggs, cookies and Cokes, Sara lay back at last to pull up sheet and quilt.

Their plan went well the next morning. Uncle Mac's letter had summoned him to New York City, and Mrs. Steiner drowned out the crackles and pops of rapidly disappearing breakfast food with the statement that she would give the house a really good cleaning.

When Sara produced the basket and asked for the raw materials of picnicking she met no opposition at all. Mrs. Steiner even made up a Thermos of frozen lemonade. Luck was on their side and it was the perfect day to go lake hunting.

Greg used a compass and led the way in what he claimed was the proper direction to reach the center of the wild gardens, but as they went the basket began to prove a nuisance. When it was necessary for the explorers to wriggle on all fours through thickets, it had to be bumped and pushed along in a way which Sara was sure mixed its contents more than was desirable. And she stoutly protested the frequent suggestions that she alone carry it, since it belonged to her anyway.

They were wrangling loudly on this point when they came, quite unexpectedly, to the top of a flight of crumbling, moss-greened stairs and saw the lake below—but not only the lake!

"It's Camelot!" Eric cried first. "Remember the picture in the Prince Valiant book? It's Camelot —King Arthur's castle!"

Sara, who had different reading tastes, dropped down on the top step and rubbed a brier-scratched hand back and forth across her knee. Her eyes were round with happy wonder as she half whispered, "Oz!"

Greg said nothing at all. It was real, it must be. And it was the most wonderful find the Lowrys had ever made. But what was it doing here and why hadn't Uncle Mac ever told them about it when he spoke of the lost lake? Who had built it and why—because real castles, even if very small ones, didn't just grow on islands in the middle of lakes these days!

Part of Uncle Mac's prophecy that the lake might be dried or drying was true. Shore marks showed it had shrunk a lot, and a stretch of sand and gravel made a bridge between the island and the shore. As he studied the building, Greg could see the castle was a ruin. Part of one tower had fallen to choke the small courtyard. But maybe they could put the stones back and rebuild it.

Excited as they all were, they descended the steps slowly. Eric looked at the murky water— it might be deeper than it looked. He hoped no one would suggest swimming, because then he might just have to try and he didn't want to, not in this lake—or, to be honest, not anywhere. He pointed into the water as he caught sight of something else. "There's a boat sunk there. Maybe they had to use that once to get to the island."

"Who built it?" Sara wondered. "There never were any knights in America. People had stopped living in castles before the Pilgrims came."

Greg teetered from heels to toes and back again. "Must have been Mr. Brosius. Maybe he came from a place where they still had castles, and wanted a little one to make him feel at home. But it's funny Uncle Mac didn't say anything about a castle here. You'd think people would remember that if they remembered the lake."

Sara picked up the basket. "Anyway we can walk right out to it now." It seemed almost as if this really were Oz and she were Dorothy approaching the Emerald City!

8

"We sure can!" Eric jumped a short space of green-scummed water, giving himself a good margin for landing on the shelf of gravel. He kicked a stone into the lake, watched the ripples lap back. Water could never be trusted, there was nothing safe or solid about it. He was very glad they had that sand-and-gravel path. This lake was unpleasantly full of shadows—shadows which might hide almost anything.

Although the castle was a miniature, it had not been built for a garrison of toy soldiers. Even Uncle Mac, tall as he was, could have passed through the front gate-way without having to stoop. But when they got beyond the pile of stones fallen from the tower, they faced a blank wall. Greg was surprised—from his survey taken from the stairs he had thought it much larger.

"What a fake!" Eric exploded. "I thought it was a real castle. It sure looked bigger from the shore."

"We can pretend it is." Sara refused to be disappointed. Even half a castle was much better than none. "If we pull all these blocks out of the way it will seem larger."

Eric kicked, sand and gravel spurting from the toe of his shoe. "Maybe."

Clearing out all those stones seemed to him a job about equal to running the lawn mower completely around the piece of garden Uncle Mac was trying to retame.

Greg moved slowly along the walls, studying the way the stones had been put together. Had the castle just been built to look pretty—something like the summer house, which was not too far from the stable yard but which they could not play in because of the rotted floor?

The part of the wall directly facing the entrance was largely concealed by a creeper that had forced its way through a crack to stretch a curtain over the stone. But when he parted those leaves in one place, he made a new discovery which suggested that his first impression of the castle's size might not have been wrong after all.

"Hey! Here's another doorway, but somebody filled it up!"

Sara's hands gripped the handles of the picnic basket so tightly that the wood cut into her palms. "Maybe—" she wet her lips "—maybe that's where he went—"

"Who went?" Eric demanded.

"Mr. Brosius—when he disappeared and they never found him at all—"

Greg laughed. "That's silly! You know what Uncle Mac said, Mr. Brosius was drowned in the river, they found his boat floating."

"But they didn't find him," Sara said stubbornly.

"No, but it was his boat and he went out in it a lot. And the river's bad along there." Greg piled up the evidence. "Remember how Mrs. Steiner harped about its being dangerous, even on the first night we came, and Uncle Mac made us promise not to go there at all?"

Eric came to Greg's support. Sure, that was the story and Mrs. Steiner had been quick to tell it to them, one of her awful warnings. Uncle Mac had even driven them down to the water and pointed out where the current was so strong and tricky. Eric shook his head to spill the picture of that rolling water out of his mind.

Last summer, and the summer before, he had had swimming lessons. And, well, it had been easy to go in with Dad, or with Slim, the instructor at the beach. But even so he didn't like or really trust a lot of water. He never had.

Maybe Greg felt the same way when he sometimes got all stiff and quiet in the dark. There was that time when they broke the flashlight going downstairs to fix a burned-out fuse and Dad had finally come down to see what was keeping them. Greg hadn't moved from the last step of the stairs at all. Well, now it wasn't dark, and they didn't have to get into the dirty old lake, so why think about things like that?

Greg was tearing away a big handful of creeper, leaving the wall bare but speckled with little patches of suckers from the vine. Whoever had sealed up that doorway long ago had been in a big hurry or careless. Because at the very top one of the filling stones was missing, leaving a dark hole.

Greg scrambled up a tottery ladder of fallen rubble and thrust his hand into the hole, which was still well above eye level.

"There's a lot of space beyond," he reported eagerly. "Maybe another room."

"Do you suppose we could pull out the rest of the stones?" Sara asked. But she was not too happy. She had not liked seeing Greg's hand disappear that way, it made her feel shivery—but excited too.

Greg was already at work, ripping free more of the creeper. Now he picked at some more of the blocks.

"Got to have something to pry this mortar loose."

None of them wanted to make the long trip back to the house for a tool. It was Eric who demanded that Sara hand over one of the forks from the picnic basket.

"They're made of stainless steel, aren't they? Well, steel's awfully tough. And anyway there're only three of us and four of them. Won't matter if we break one."

Sara protested hotly, but she did want to see what lay behind the wall and finally she handed over a fork. The boys took turns picking out crumbling mortar and, as the fork did the job very easily, they were able to pass the loose stones to their sister to stack to one side. Midges buzzed about, and some very hungry mosquitoes decided it was lunch time. Spiders, large, hairy, and completely horrible, ran from disturbed homes in the creeper and made Sara a little sick as they scuttled madly by.

At last Greg pulled up to look through the irregular window they had cleared.

"What's inside?" Sara jerked at Greg's dangling shirt tail and Eric clamored to be allowed to take his place.

There was an odd expression on Greg's tanned face.

13

"Answer a person, can't you? What's there?"

"I don't know—"

"Let me see!" Eric applied an elbow to good purpose and took his brother's place.

"Why, it's all gray!" he cried out a moment later. "Maybe just a sealed-up room without any windows—the kind to keep treasure in. Maybe this is where Mr. Brosius kept all his gold."

The thought of possible treasure banished some of Sara's doubts. It also spurred the boys on to harder efforts and they soon had a larger space cleared so Sara could see in too.

It *was* gray in there, as if the space on the other side of the wall were full of fog. She did not like it, but if it was a treasure place . . . Mr. Brosius had always spent gold in the village. That story was true; people still talked about it a lot.

"I'm the oldest." Greg broke the silence with an assertion that had led them into—and sometimes out of—trouble many times in the past. "I'll go first."

He climbed over the few remaining stones and was gone. It seemed to Sara that the gray stuff inside had wrapped right around him.

"Greg!" she cried, but Eric was already pushing past her.

"Here goes!" As usual he refused to admit that a year's difference in age meant any difference in daring, strength, or the ability to take care of oneself under difficulties. He also vanished.

14

Sara gulped, and backed away a step or two from that grayness. Her foot struck against the picnic basket and she caught at the double handles, lifted it over the barrier, and scrambled after, determined not to lose the boys.

Beyond the Wall

It was like walking into the heart of a cloud, though the gray stuff about Sara was neither cold nor wet. But to be unable to see her feet or her hands, or anything but the whirling mist, made her dizzy. She shut her eyes as she stumbled forward.

"Greg! Eric!" She had meant to shout at the top of her voice, but the names sounded like weak whispers. She choked, shivered, and began to run, the basket bumping awkwardly against her legs.

There was a bird singing somewhere and the ground underfoot felt different. Sara slowed down, then stood still and opened her eyes.

The fog was gone. But where was she? Surely not inside a room of the small castle. Timidly she reached out to touch a tree trunk and found it to be real. Then she looked back for the wall and the door. Trees, just more trees, all huge and old with thick mats of dead leaves brown and soft under them. And sunshine coming through in ragged patches.

"Eric! Greg!" Sara was screaming and she did not care. Now her voice sounded properly loud once more.

Something stepped into the open from behind a tree trunk. Sara's mouth was open for another shout. A red-brown, black, and white animal with a plumed tail and a thin, pointed nose sat

down to look at her with interest. Sara stared back. Her fright was fading fast, and she was sure that the animal was laughing at her. Now she knew it was a fox. Only, she was puzzled. Were foxes always so big? The ones she had seen in the zoo were much, much smaller. This one was as large as the Great Dane that had lived two houses away on the post in Colorado. He was very like, she decided, the picture of Rollicum-Bitem in *Midnight Folk,* a favorite fictional person of hers.

"Hello," she ventured.

The fox's mouth opened and his pointy tongue showed a little. Then he snapped at an impudent fly. Sara put down the basket. Would he like a peanut butter sandwich? There *were* the cold ham ones, but only three of them. Before she could move, the fox stood up and with a flick of his plumed tail was gone.

"Sara! Where are you, Sara?"

Greg dodged in and out among the trees. When he caught sight of her he waved impatiently. "Come on. We've found a river!"

Sara sighed as she picked up the basket again. She was sure that the fox wouldn't come back, not with Greg yelling that way. Then she began to wonder about the river. What was a river doing on a small island? When they had seen that dab of land from the top of the stairs, there had not been any big trees or river.

As she caught up with Greg she asked, "Where

are we, Greg? How did all these trees and a river get on a small island?"

He looked puzzled too. "I don't know. I don't think we're on the island any more, Sara." He took the basket from her and clasped her arm above the elbow with his other hand. "Come on. You'll see what I mean when you get there."

They trotted in and out among the trees, which then grew farther and farther apart, and there was a lot of green-gold sunlight in the open spaces with grass and little plants.

"Butterflies! I've never seen so many butter-flies!" Sara dragged back against her brother's pull. What she had first thought were flowers rose on brilliant wings to fly away.

"Yes." Greg walked more slowly. "A lot of birds here, too. You ought to see them down by the river. There was a heron fishing and we watched him catch a frog." He made a stabbing motion with two fingers held tightly together. "He used his bill just like that. This is a grand place."

They walked down a gentle slope to where a bar of gravel ran out into a shallow stream. Eric sprawled there, grabbing beneath the surface of the water. He sat up, his face red with his efforts, as they joined him.

"Fish," he explained. "All over the place. Just look at them!"

Shoals of minnows were thick along the edges of the bar, while water bugs skated on the sur-face and a dragonfly spun back and forth.

"I saw a fox in the woods," Sara reported. "He sat and looked at me and wasn't afraid at all. But where are we?"

Eric rolled over on his back, looking up into the blue of the cloudless sky, still dabbling one hand in the river.

"I don't care. This is a keen place, better than any old park—or any old scout camp either," he added for Greg's benefit. "And now I'm hungry. Let's see what's in that basket we've been hauling around all morning."

They moved into the shade of a stand of willows where the slightest breeze set the narrow leaves to fluttering. Sara unpacked the basket. It was Greg who pointed out that she was counting wrong.

"Hey—there're only three of us. Why put out everything for four?"

Yes, she had put out all four of the plastic plates, set a cup beside each, and had been dividing up the sandwiches. Greg had the red plate, Eric the yellow, the blue was for her. Why had she set out the green one also? Yet for some reason she was sure that it would be needed. "We may have a guest," she said.

"What do you mean? There's no one here but us." Eric laughed at her.

Sara sat back on her heels. "All right, Mr. Smarty," she snapped. "Suppose you tell me where we really are, if you know so much! This is no little island in the lake, you can't make me believe that! How do you know there's no one else here?"

Eric stopped laughing. He looked uncertainly from his sister to Greg. Then all three of them glanced back at the shadowy wood through which they had come. Greg drew a deep breath and Sara spoke again:

"And how are we going to get back? Has either of you big smart boys thought of that?" She reached for the basket as if touching that would link her with the real world again.

Greg frowned at the river. "We can get back to where we came from," he said. "I blazed trees between here and there with my scout knife." Sara was surprised and then proud of him. Greg had been clever to think of that. And, knowing that they had that tie with the castle wall and its door, she felt more at ease. But now she gathered up a sandwich from each plate and returned them to the basket. If Greg could think ahead, so could she.

"Hey!" Eric's protest was quick and sharp. "Why are you putting those away? I'm hungry!"

"You might be hungrier," she countered, "if we don't get back in time for supper."

Greg was unscrewing the top of the Thermos when he suddenly got to his feet, looking at a point behind Sara. The expression on his face made Sara turn and stopped Eric in mid-chew.

As silently as the fox had appeared back in the forest, so now did another being come into view.

22

And, while Sara had accepted the fox as a proper
native of the woods, none of the Lowrys had ever
seen a man quite like this one.

He was young, Sara thought, but a lot older
than Greg. And he had a nice face, even a hand-
some one, though it wore a tired, sad look. His
brown hair, which had red lights in it under the
sun's touch, was long, the side locks almost touching his shoulders, the front part cut off in thick
straight bangs above his black eyebrows.

Then his clothes! He had on tight-fitting boots
of soft brown leather with pointed toes, and he
wore what looked like long stockings—tights,
maybe—also brown. Over his shirt he had a
sleeveless garment of the same green as the tree
leaves, with a design embroidered in gold on the
breast; it was drawn in tightly at the waist by a
wide belt from which hung a sheathed dagger
and a purse. In his hand was a long bow with
which he was holding back the willow branches
while he looked at the Lowrys in an astonishment
that matched their own.

Sara got to her feet, brushing twigs and dust
from her jeans.

"Please, sir—" she added the "sir" because
somehow it seemed right and proper, just as if
the stranger were the colonel back at the post
"—will you have some lunch?"

The young man still looked bewildered. But
the faint frown he had first worn was gone.

24

"Lunch?" He echoed the word inquiringly, giving the word a different accent.

Eric gulped down what was in his mouth and waved at the plates. "Food!"

"Yes," Sara stooped for the green plate and held it out in invitation. "Do open the lemonade, Greg, before Eric chokes to death." For that last bite appeared to have taken the wrong way down Eric's throat and he was coughing.

Suddenly the young man laughed and came forward. He leaned down to strike Eric between his shaking shoulders. The boy whooped and then swallowed, his eyes watering. Greg splashed lemonade into a cup and thrust it toward his brother.

"Greedy!" he accused. "Next time don't try to get half a sandwich in one bite." He squatted down to fill the other three cups and pushed the green one toward the stranger.

Their guest took the cup, turning it around in his fingers as though he found the plastic substance strange. Then he sipped at the contents.

"A strange wine," he commented. "It cools the throat well, but it seems to be squeezed of grapes grown in snow."

"It isn't wine, sir," Sara hastened to explain. "Just lemonade—the frozen kind. These are peanut butter," she pointed to the sandwiches. "And that one is ham. Then there're hard-boiled eggs and pickles and some cookies—Mrs. Steiner does make good cookies."

The young man regarded all the food on his plate in a puzzled manner and finally picked up the egg.

"Salt—" Greg pushed the shaker across.

Eric had stopped coughing, though he was still red in the face. Somehow he found breath enough to ask a question.

"Do you live around here, sir?"

"Live here? No, not this nigh to the boundary. You are not of this land?"

"We came through a gate in a wall," Greg explained. "There was a castle—"

"A little castle on an island," Sara broke in. "And in the wall was this gate, all filled up with stones. The boys pulled those out so we could get through."

He was giving her the same searching attention he had given the food. "The boys?" he repeated wonderingly, "but are you not all three boys?"

Sara looked from her brothers to herself. Their jeans did all look alike, so did their shirts. But her hair—no, her hair wasn't even as long as the young man's.

"I'm Sara Lowry, and I'm a girl," she stated a bit primly, for the first time in her life annoyed at being considered one with Greg and Eric, a mistake she had hitherto always rather enjoyed. "That's my older brother, Greg." She pointed with a total lack of good manners. "And this is Eric."

The young man put his hand to his breast and bowed. It was a graceful gesture and did not in

26

the least make Sara feel queer or foolish, but rather as if she were important and grown-up.

"And I am Huon, Warden of the West." His forefinger traced the design pictured in gold thread on his green surcoat. Sara saw the scales of a coiled dragon with menacing foreclaws and wide-open jaws. "The Green Dragon—as Arthur is the Red Dragon of the East."

Greg laid down the sandwich he had been about to unwrap. He stared very hard at Huon and there was a stubborn line to his lips—the way he looked when he thought someone was trying to make fun of him.

"You mean Arthur Pendragon. But that's a story—a fairy tale!"

"Arthur Pendragon," the young man nodded encouragingly. "So you have heard of the Red Dragon, then? But not the green one?"

"Huon—there was Huon of the Horn." To Sara's vast surprise Eric said that. "And I suppose Roland's back in there?" He pointed to the wood.

But now the young man shook his head and his smile vanished.

"No. Roland fell at Roncesvalles long before my wardship here began. I wish we *did* have his like to back us now. But you have named me rightly, young sir. Once I was Huon of the Horn. Now I am Huon without the Horn, which is a bad thing. But still I am Warden of the West and so must inquire of you your business here. This gate through which you came—I do not under-

stand," he added as if to himself. "There has been
no summoning on our part. That portal was made
and then sealed when Ambrosius returned to us
with the knowledge that our worlds had moved
too far away in space and time for men to answer
our calling. Yet you have come——" Now he was
frowning again. "Can it be that here also the
enemy meddles?"

"I wish somebody would explain," Sara said
in a small voice. More than ever she wanted to
know where they were. It seemed that the young
man understood, for now he spoke directly to her:

"This land"——his hand made a wide sweep——
"once had four gates. That of the Bear in the
north has long been lost to us, for the enemy has
occupied the land where it exists for a wealth of
years. That of the Lion in the south we have
closed with a powerful spell so that it is safe.
That of the Boar, which lay in the east, has been
forgotten so long that even Merlin Ambrosius
cannot tell us where it was——or may still be. And
that of the Fox here in the west. Some years ago
Merlin reopened that, only to discover that there
was no longer any way he could touch men's
minds. Then did our fears grow——" Huon paused
and sat looking down into his cup, not as if he
saw the lemonade there, but other things, and
unpleasant ones. "And the door was sealed——until
you opened it." He fell silent.

"I saw a fox there," Sara did not quite know
why she said that.

Huon smiled at her. "Yes, Rufus is a good sentinel. He marked your coming and summoned me. The creatures of the wood aid us gladly, since our lives move along the same paths."

"But what is this country and who are the enemy?" Greg asked impatiently.

"The country has many names in your world —Avalon, Awanan, Atlantis—almost as many names as there were men to name it. Have you never heard of it before? Surely you must if you know also the tale of Arthur Pendragon!" He inclined his head courteously to Greg. "And of me, Huon, once of the Horn. For this is the land to which both Arthur and I were summoned. Or is that now forgot in the world of men?" He ended a little sadly.

Arthur Pendragon—that was King Arthur of the Round Table, Sara now remembered. But Huon—she did not know his story and wished she could ask Eric about him.

Greg was scowling not at Huon but at the ground between his feet where he was digging holes with one of the spoons from the basket.

"It's completely cockeyed," he muttered. "King Arthur is just a legend. The real Arthur, he was a British-Roman who fought the Saxons. He never had a Round Table or any knights! Mr. Legard told us all about him in history last term. The rest of it—the Round Table and the knights— that was all made up in the Middle Ages, stories they told at feasts—like TV."

Huon shook his head. "Story or not in your world, young sir, you are now truly in Avalon this day. Just as I am eating your food and drinking this strange but refreshing wine of yours. And Rufus passed you through the Gate of the Fox without challenge. Thus it is meant that you should come here."

Cold Iron

"That you have come through our gate without hurt or challenge," Huon continued, "means that you have not been sent or called by them." He held up his hand in a swift sign the children did not understand.

"Them?" Sara asked before biting into her sandwich. This talk about a gate was reassuring because they could go back the same way they had come through.

"The enemy," Huon replied, "are those powers of darkness who war against all that is good and fair and right. Wizards of the Black, witches, warlocks, werewolves, ghouls, ogres—the enemy has as many names and faces as Avalon itself —many bodies and disguises, some fair, but mainly foul. They are shadows of the darkness, who have long sought to overwhelm Avalon and then win to victory in other worlds, yours among them. Think of what you fear and hate the most, and that will be a part of the enemy and the Dark Powers.

"We lie in danger here, for by spells and treachery three talismans have been lost to us: Excalibur, Merlin's ring, and the horn—all within three days' time. And if we go into battle without them—ah, ah—" Huon shook his head "—we shall be as men fighting with weighty chains loaded upon arms and limbs." Then abruptly he asked a question: "Do you have the privilege of cold iron?"

As they stared at him in bewilderment, he pointed to one of the basket knives. "Of what metal is this wrought?"

"Stainless steel," Greg replied. "But what has that got to do with—?"

"Stainless steel," Huon interrupted. "But you have no iron—cold iron—forged by a mortal in the world of mortals? Or do you have the need for silver also?"

"We do have some silver," Sara volunteered. She brought out from the breast pocket of her shirt the knotted handkerchief which held the rest of the week's allowance, a dime and a quarter.

"What's all this about iron and silver?" Eric wanted to know.

"This." Huon drew the dagger from his belt sheath. In the shade of the willows the blade shone as brightly as if he held it in the direct sunlight. And when he turned it the metal gave off flashes of fire, as a burning log might spit sparks. "This is dwarf-forged silver—not cold iron. For one who is of Avalon may not hold an iron blade within his hand lest he be burnt flesh and bone."

Greg held up the spoon with which he had been digging. "Steel *is* iron, but I'm not burned."

"Ah," Huon smiled, "but you are not truly of Avalon. As I am not, as Arthur is not. Once I swung a sword of iron, went battle clad in iron mail. But here in Avalon I laid aside such gear lest it do sad hurt to those who follow me. So I bear a dwarf-made silver blade and wear silver armor, as does Arthur. To the elf kind, cold iron is a breaker of good spells, a poison giving deep, unhealing hurts. In all of Avalon, there were once only two pieces of true iron. And now those have been taken from us—perhaps to our undoing." He twirled the flickering dagger between his fingers so that sparks dazzled their eyes.

"What are the two pieces of iron you lost?" Sara wanted to know.

"You have heard of the sword Excalibur?"

"Arthur's sword—the one he pulled from the rock," supplied Greg and then saw that Huon was gently laughing at him.

"But Arthur is only a story, have you not said so? Yet it seems to me that you know much of that story."

33

"Sure," Eric said impatiently, "everybody knows about King Arthur and his sword. Gee, I read about that when I was just a little kid. But that doesn't make it true," he ended a little belligerently.

"And Excalibur was one of the things you lost?" Sara persisted.

"Not lost. As I said, it was stolen through a spell and hidden by another which Merlin cannot break. Excalibur has vanished, and Merlin's ring —that was also a thing of iron and of great power—for its wearer may command beast and bird, tree and earth. The sword, the ring, and the horn—"

"Was that iron, too?"

"No. But it is a thing of sorcery, given to me by the elf king Oberon, once high lord in this land. It can both aid and destroy. Once it nearly destroyed me, many times it came to my aid. But now I am without the Horn, and much of my power has departed—which may be an ill, ill thing for Avalon!"

"Who stole them?" Eric asked.

"The enemy, who else? They gather all their strength now to come down upon us and with their witchery nibble away at all our safeguards. It was laid upon Avalon at the Dawn of All that this land was to stand as a wall between the dark and your own mortal world. When we drive back the dark and hold it firmly in check, then peace reigns in your world. But let the dark surge forward here, winning victories, then in turn you know troubles, wars, evil.

"Avalon and your world are mirrors for each other in some fashion even beyond the understanding of Merlin Ambrosius, who knows the heart of Avalon and is the greatest one ever to be born of mortal woman and elf king. What chances with us must follow with you. And now the dark rises high. First it seeped in silently, an almost unmarked flood, now they dare to challenge us to open combat. But with our talisman gone what man—or wizard—can foresee what will chance with Avalon and her sister world?"

"And why did you want to know if we could handle iron?" asked Greg.

For a moment Huon hesitated, while his gaze went from the boys to Sara. Then he drew a deep breath as if he were about to dive into a pool.

"When one comes through the gates, it is because he has been summoned and some destiny awaits him here. Only a very great magic can reopen the way for him to go forth from Avalon again. And cold iron is your magic, just as we have other sorcery for ours."

Eric jumped to his feet. "I don't believe it. It's all a made-up story and we're going right back where we came from. Come on, Greg—Sara— let's go!"

Greg rose slowly, Sara did not move at all. Eric pulled at his brother's arm. "You blazed the

trail from the gate, didn't you?" he shouted.
"Show me where. Come on, Sara!"

She was repacking the basket. "All right. You
go on."

Eric turned and ran. Sara looked straight into
Huon's brown eyes. "The gate is really closed,
isn't it?" she asked. "We can't go away again until
your magic lets us, can we?" She did not know
how she knew that, but Sara was sure she spoke
the truth.

"I have naught to do with it." Huon sounded
sad. "Though I have powers of a sort, none of
them controls the gates. I believe that not even
Merlin can open them for you—if you have been
summoned—only when *you* make your choice—"

Greg moved closer. "What choice? You mean
we have to stay here until we do something?
What? Maybe get back Excalibur, or that ring,
or the horn?"

Huon shrugged. "It is not for me to say. Only
in Caer Siddi, the Castle Foursquare, may we
learn the truth."

"Is that a long way from here?" Sara wanted
to know.

"If one goes afoot, perhaps. For the Horse of
the Hills it is no journey at all."

Huon stepped from the shade of the willows
into the open sun of the river bank. He put his
fingers to his mouth and blew a shrill whistle.

He was answered from the sky overhead. Sara
watched with round eyes and Greg cried out.

36

There was a splash, as water washed about hoofs, and the flapping of huge wings. Two black horses stood in the shallow river, the cool water eddying about their legs. But such horses! Ribbed wings like those of bats were folded against their powerful shoulders as they shook their heads and neighed a welcome to the man who had summoned them. They wore neither saddle nor bridle, but it was clear they had come to serve Huon.

One bent its head to drink, snuffling into the water, raising again a dripping muzzle. The other trotted to the bank and stretched out his head toward Greg, eying the boy with what could only be intelligent interest.

"This is Khem and that is Sitta." As Huon spoke their names, both horses bowed their heads and whinnied gently. "The paths of the upper air are as well known to them as the roads of earth. And they will bear us to Caer Siddi before sundown."

"Greg! Sara!" That was Eric shouting as he burst from the grove. "There's no gate. I followed the blazes back—no gate—only two trees standing close together!"

"Did I not say the time for return is not yet?" Huon nodded. "You must find the right key for that."

Sara gripped the basket tightly. She had believed that from the first. But somehow, to have Eric say it was sobering.

"All right." Greg faced the winged horses.

37

"Let's get going then. I want to find out about the key and how to get home again."

Eric fell in step beside Sara, banging his hand against the basket. "You can't drag that along, too. Leave it here."

Huon came to her aid. "The maid is wise, Eric. For this is also one of the spells of Avalon: those who eat entirely of her food, drink only her wines and water, cannot easily escape her borders once again, unless they take upon themselves some grave change. Treasure the rest of your food and drink and add it to ours when you break your fast."

Greg and Eric mounted on Sitta, Eric's arms tight about his brother's waist, Greg's hands twined in the horse's mane. Huon took Sara up before him on Khem. The horses began to trot and then to gallop and their wings snapped open. Then they were mounting up above the sunlit water and the lacy green of the trees.

Khem circled once and headed southeast, Sitta matching him wing to wing. A flock of large black birds started up from a field and flew with them for a while, calling in cracked, shrill voices, until the horses outdistanced them.

At first Sara was afraid to look earthward. In fact she shut her eyes tight, glad of Huon's arm about her, the solid wall of his body at her back. It made her giddy to think of what lay beneath . . . and then she heard Huon laugh.

"Come, Lady Sara, this is not so ill a way to travel. Men have long envied birds their freedom of wings, and this is the nearest mortals can come to such flight, unless they be under some enchantment and no longer men. I would not trust you to some colt fresh out of the cloud pastures. But Khem is a steady mount and will not play us any tricks. Is that not so, Father of Swift Runners?"

The horse neighed and Sara dared to open her eyes. It was really not so bad to watch the passing of the green countryside. Then from ahead there was a flash of light, rather like the sparks from Huon's dagger, but much, much larger. It was sun reflected from the roofs of four tall towers linked in a square by walls of gray-green stone.

"That is Caer Siddi, the Castle Foursquare, which is the western hold of Avalon, as Camelot is the eastern. Ha, Khem, take care in your landing, I see a muster within the walls!"

They circled well above the four towers of the outer keep and Sara looked down. People were moving below. A banner flapped from the tallest tower, a green bannner of the same color as Huon's surcoat, and worked upon it in gold was a dragon.

Tall walls rose about them, and Sara shut her eyes again quickly. Then Huon's arm tightened, and Khem was trotting, not flying. They were on the ground.

People crowded around, so many of them that at first Sara noticed only their odd dress. She stood on the pavement, glad when Greg and Eric joined her.

"Boy, oh boy, some way to travel!" Eric burst out. "Bet a jet would beat 'em, though!"

Greg was more interested in what lay about them now. "Archers! Just look at those bows!"

Sara followed her brother's direction. The archers were dressed alike, much the same as Huon. But they also wore shirts of many silvery rings linked together and over those, gray surcoats with green and gold dragons on the breasts. Their silver helmets fitted down about their faces so that it was hard to see their features. Each carried a bow as tall as himself, and slung across one shoulder was an arrow-filled quiver.

Beyond the lines of archers were more men. They, too, had ringed shirts and dragon-marked surcoats. But long green cloaks fastened at their throats. And instead of bows they had swords belted about them, while their helmets were topped with small green plumes.

Behind the men with the swords were the ladies. Sara became acutely conscious of her jeans, of the shirt which had been clean that morning but was now dirty and torn. No wonder Huon had believed her to be a boy if this was the way women dressed in Avalon! Most of them had long plaits of hair with sparkling threads braided into them. And the flower-colored dresses were long with gemmed girdles at the waists,

while their loose sleeves hung in points to touch the ground.

One of the ladies, her hair dark and curling about her face, her blue-green dress rippling about her as she moved, came toward them. She had a circlet of gold and pearl on her head, and the others made way for her as if she were a queen.

"Lady of Avalon," Huon came up to her, "these are three who have entered through the Fox Gate, by let and with no hindrance. This is the Lady Sara, and her brothers Greg and Eric. And this is the Lady Claramonde who is my wife, and so High Lady of Avalon."

Just to say "hello" seemed wrong somehow. Sara smiled timidly and the lady smiled back. Then the lady's hands were on Sara's shoulders and, because the lady was small, she had only to stoop a little to kiss the girl on the forehead.

"Welcome, three times welcome." The Lady Claramonde smiled again and then turned to Eric, flustering him greatly by greeting him with the same kiss, before facing Greg. "May you all rest well within these walls. And peace be yours."

"Thanks," Eric blurted out. But to Sara's astonishment Greg made a quite creditable bow and seemed very pleased with himself.

There was another personage to greet them. The crowd of knights and archers opened a path for him as the ladies had done for Claramonde. Only this was no man-of-arms who walked toward them, but a tall person in a plain gray robe on which lines of red twisted and coiled in strange patterns. His hair was as gray as his robe and lay on his shoulders in thick locks which mingled on his breast with the wide spread of his beard. He had the brightest eyes Sara had ever seen—eyes which made one think he was looking straight into one's mind and reading everything which lay there, good or bad.

For a belt he had a sash of the same dull red as the patterns on his robe. And when one watched it closely it appeared to move, as if it possessed some strange life of its own.

"So at long last they have come." He surveyed the Lowrys with a somewhat stern look.

Sara was uncomfortable at first, but when those dark eyes were turned directly upon her she lost her fear, if not her awe. She had never seen anyone like this man before, but she was sure he meant her no ill. In fact, quite the contrary, something reached out from him to her, giving her confidence, taking away the faint uneasiness which had been with her ever since she had passed through the gate.

"Yes, Merlin, they have come. For good reasons, let us hope, for good." Huon's voice was low and Sara thought that he too, for all his lordship, looked upon Merlin as someone greater and wiser than he.

Merlin's Mirror

"I don't like this. We've got to get away before something happens." Eric was looking out of one of the narrow castle windows. "It can't be far from sundown. What'll happen if we don't get back to Uncle Mac's for supper?"

Sara, seated on a velvet-cushioned stool, the picnic basket between her feet, laughed. "Mrs. Steiner will have a fit, that's what. Anyway Huon and Lady Claramonde are nice and I don't think they'd let anything bad happen. And how would we get back with the gate gone? Besides, that's miles and miles away from here and we don't know the way back."

"No? Well, I bet those flying horses know it. We could get a couple of them and—"

"And how are you going to do that?" Greg

came out of the shadows at the door of the chamber. "There're umpteen people around and they'd ask questions if we tried to walk out. Also, what makes you think the horses would fly for us? Sara's right, what would be the use of going back to the gate anyway, if it's no longer there?"

Greg was no taller than he had been that morning. There was a smudge of dirt on his chin, and his thick light hair needed combing. But he was different, maybe different inside, Sara thought. When he talked quietly like that, he sounded almost like Father in a serious mood.

"You mean we have to stay here until they let us go?" Eric exploded.

Sara turned on him indignantly. "That's not fair and you know it, Eric Lowry! They're not keeping us prisoner. Didn't Huon tell us right at the start that he had no way of opening the gate for us?"

Eric strode over to stand before her, his hands on his hips. "And you're ready to believe everything they tell you!"

"Be quiet!" Greg cut in, sounding more like Father than ever. Eric half swung around ready for an angry retort, but his brother continued, "Sara's right. If part of what they've told us is true, all must be. We are in a castle, aren't we? A regular King Arthur castle. And how did we get here, by riding on a pair of winged horses. Also," he ended thoughtfully, "Merlin is no hoax. And he said he had to talk with us."

"I don't trust him either!" Eric snapped defiantly.

"So, you do not trust me, young sir?"

Sara started and Eric jumped. They had been facing the room's one doorway, but they had not seen Merlin enter. Only now he was standing there, his bright eyes on them.

"Eric didn't mean that," Sara began hastily.

"Oh, but I think he did." Merlin combed his beard with the fingers of his right hand, while those of his left patted his sash belt. In the stone-walled room he seemed even taller than he had in the courtyard, and the gray of his robe blended into the gray of the walls until he might have been part of the castle itself. Now he seated himself in a high-backed chair and surveyed the Lowrys as they stood uneasily before him.

"Eric is entirely right," Merlin continued after a pause during which their discomfort grew. "Yes, he is entirely right not to trust me, Sara."

"Why?"

"Because to me the good of Avalon lies above all else. For more years than there are blocks in these walls about us, I have been one of the three guardians of this land. Arthur wields sword, mace, and lance in the east, Huon stands with his elf knights, a wall of fighting men, in the west. And I bend other powers and forces to strengthen them both. It was not so long ago that I crossed the gulf of time and space to open the Fox Gate—I,

Merlin Ambrosius, the only man to walk that way in a long tale of centuries."

"Then you're Mr. Brosius!" Greg interrupted.

Merlin pulled at his beard. "So, I am still remembered? Time is not so well matched between our worlds—here it flows much faster than in yours. Yes, I opened the gate and sought those who would aid us in the coming struggle. But," his voice sounded sad now, "there were none of the right spirit and mind, none we could summon as once the powers of this land summoned Arthur and Huon and me. Now it seems the gate has done its own selecting, just as we face a newer, stronger attack from the forces of evil."

"Huon told us about losing Excalibur, your ring, and the horn," Greg said.

"So?" Merlin's bushy eyebrows lifted. "Then you can understand why we are so excited at your coming. We lose three talismans, and then you arrive. What else can we believe but that your fate is tied to our loss?"

"We didn't steal your things!" Eric sputtered.

"That we know. But you may aid in their return, if you will."

"And if we don't—then you won't let us go home again—that's it, isn't it?" Eric demanded rudely.

Merlin only looked at him and Eric flushed. It was Greg's turn to ask:

"*Is* that true, sir? We can't go home?"

Merlin was quiet again for a long moment, and

48

suddenly Sara had a queer shamed feeling, as if she had done something wrong, although she had not spoken at all. And Eric's face was now very red.

"There is a spell which will force the gate open, yes. If you truly wish that."

"But you believe that we were meant to come here to help you, don't you, sir?" Greg persisted.

Merlin nodded. About his waist the colored lines of his sash twisted and spun until they made Sara so dizzy she had to close her eyes and turn her head away.

"You have a choice, young sirs, Lady Sara. But I must also tell you that, if you choose to give us your aid, the roads set by the mirror are never easy to follow, and he or she who travels them does not return unchanged from such journeying."

"Is it also true that when your enemy here wins a battle, then our world is endangered too?" Greg continued.

Again Merlin inclined his head. "Does your world now rest easy, my son? For the evil tide has been rising here, growing ever stronger through the years. I ask you again, does your world rest easy nowadays?"

Sara shivered. She was not quite sure what Merlin meant. But she remembered all the talk back on the other side of the gate, the things she had heard Mother and Father say.

"No," that was Greg answering, "there's always talk about another war and the Bomb."

"Avalon still holds fast, though how long we may continue to do so"—Merlin's eyes were so bright it hurt to look at them, Sara thought—"no man, mortal or elf kind, can say. It is your choice to aid us or no."

"Dad's a soldier in our world," Greg said slowly. "And if another war comes—the one everyone has been afraid of—would it come there if the enemy wins here, sir?"

"The enemy is never wholly defeated, neither in Avalon nor in your world," Merlin sighed. "He wears many surcoats, marches under many different banners, but he always exists. It is our hope to keep him ever on the defensive, always to face him squarely and never allow him a full victory. Yes, if he wins here, then well may he win in your time and space also."

"Then I choose to do as you wish," Greg answered. "It's for Dad, in a way." He looked questioningly at Sara and Eric.

"All right." Eric's agreement was reluctant. He looked as scared and unhappy as Sara felt inside.

She held to the basket which was the only real thing now in this mixed-up dream. And her voice was very small and thin as she said, "Me, I'll help too," though she did not want to at all.

Merlin straightened in his chair and now he was

smiling. Sara was warmer, seeing that smile, and almost happy.

"Then do you search out our talismans, where-soever they may lie and whosoever may guard them. Remember, cold iron is your servant and your magic—call upon it when you must—and change is the pattern of your going. And the time to begin is now!"

His voice rang as loud as a trumpet blast. Sara cried out as she had when the gate mist had wrapped her in. Then the roaring was gone.

They were still three together. She caught Eric's and Greg's hands. Neither boy pulled away from her. But this was a new place—there were no windows in this room and the light came from five globes of pale green fire set in a star overhead. Three of the walls were covered with hangings of cloth such as Sara had once seen in a museum. There were pictures on the cloth, which moved as if a current of air blew behind it. Strange men with hairy legs ran races there with unicorns. Birds flew and the leaves of the trees seemed to rustle, or perhaps it was the air which made that sound.

The fourth wall was very different, a vast shin-ing surface reflecting all within the room. Of Merlin there was no sign. Sara's grip on her brothers' hands tightened. Now she wished they had asked to go home.

"I don't like this place," she cried and the words re-echoed—"place-place-place."

Greg pulled free and walked to the mirror wall. When he stood before it, he put out his hands so they lay palm flat on its surface. The other two followed him hesitantly.

"Greg, what do you see?" Sara crowded in on one side, Eric on the other. Both of them looked over his shoulders into the strip bordered by his hand.

They might have been looking through a window out upon open countryside. Only what lay beyond was not the green and gold land over which the winged horses had carried them, but a very different country.

Nor was it day, but night. Moonlight showed a wandering road just outside, climbing up and up until it was lost to sight on a mountainside. It was bordered by thickets of stunted trees, most of them leafless, and many of them twisted into queer, frightening shapes so their shadows on the ground looked like goblins or monsters. That was all—just a white road running on into dark and gloomy mountains.

"This is the road for Greg. Let him arm himself with cold iron and go!"

Was that order voiced by the people of the tapestry, or did it come from the air?

"No!" Sara cried out. "Eric, stop him!" She tried to hold Greg's arm. "It's so dark." Greg hated dark—maybe that would stop him.

But for the second time he broke her hold.

"Don't be silly! If we want to help, we'll have to follow orders."

"That's a bad place, Greg. I know it is!" She turned to look at the road again. It was gone and in the mirror she could see only the reflection of the room and the three Lowrys.

"Arm himself with cold iron," Eric repeated, puzzled.

"Cold iron." Greg went down on one knee beside the picnic basket. "Remember what Huon told us about the power of iron. The same thing must be true of steel." He opened the basket to show the forks, the knives, and the spoons.

Sara sat down beside him, trying hard not to show her fright.

"Remember what he said about the magic in the food also? That we must always eat some of our own along with theirs? You must take something to eat." Her hands were shaking as she put a sandwich, an egg, and some cookies into a napkin and made it into a packet. Greg took one of the forks from the webbing.

"You call that a weapon?" Eric jeered. "I think you'd better ask for a sword, or one of those big bows. After all, if you're going to help Avalon, they ought to give you something better."

"Cold iron, remember? And this is pointed, sharp." He tested the tines on his finger. "This is what I'm to take, I knew it the minute I touched it. Thanks for the food, Sara."

With the napkin packet in one hand and the

fork in the other, Greg walked once more to the mirror.

"Hey, Greg, wait a minute!" Eric tried to intercept him and Sara cried out a despairing "Greg!" But at the same time she knew her protest was useless, for Greg was wearing his "do-it-now-and-get-it-over-with" expression.

They reached the mirror too late. Greg had already touched its surface. He was gone—though Sara believed that she saw for an instant a shadowy figure on the mountain road.

Eric ran his hands over the surface through which Greg had vanished. He pounded on it with his fists.

"Greg!" he shouted, and the tapestries stirred, but there was nothing to be seen now but the reflection of their two selves. Sara went back to the basket and then heard an exclamation from Eric.

As his brother had done before him, he was leaning close to the glass, his hands flat against it. And he was watching something.

"Is it Greg? Can you see him?" Sara flew to the mirror. Maybe they could go through, be with Greg—

But over Eric's shoulder she saw no moonlit road or high mountains. Instead there was a stretch of seashore, a beach of sand, with tufts of coarse grass in dark green blots. White birds coasted over the rolling waves and it was day, not night.

"This is the road for Eric. Let him arm himself with cold iron and go!"

Were those Merlin's words? Both children pushed back from the mirror. Sara looked at her brother. He was chewing his lower lip, staring down at his hands.

"Are you going?" she asked in a small voice.

He scowled and kicked at the basket. "Greg went, didn't he? If he can do it, then I can—I will! Give me some food, too, Sara, and one of those forks."

But when he took the fork, he hesitated, and slowly slid it back into the webbing loop again.

"That doesn't feel right," he said. Even more slowly he pulled out the spoon in the next loop. "This is better. Why?"

"Maybe you take what is going to help you most," suggested Sara. She was making up a second packet of food. Though she wanted to beg Eric not to go, she knew that she could not keep him from this adventure, not after he had watched Greg go before him.

"Good luck," she said forlornly as he took the food.

Eric was still scowling as he faced the mirror and his only answer was a shrug. "This is crazy," he complained. "Well, here goes!"

As Greg had done, he walked to the mirror and through it. Sara was left sitting on the floor in a very empty room.

She studied the mirror. It had made a door for

Greg, another for Eric. And she knew it was only waiting to make a door for her.

"I wish we could all have gone together," she said aloud, and then she wished she had not, for the echoes rang until it sounded like people whispering behind the tapestry.

Sara picked up the basket and went to the mirror. Then she said determinedly:

"Show me my road, I am ready to go."

There was no mirror at all, but green and gold and sunshine. She marched ahead and her feet passed from floor to the softness of earth. For a moment Sara was bewildered. Here was no mountain road, no seashore. She was in the middle of a woodland glade. Could it be the same wood as held the gate?

This was so different from Greg's dark and lonesome road, from the wild seashore where Eric had gone, that Sara could not help being a little cheered. Only now that she was here, what was she to do?

"Kaaaw—"

Sara looked up. On a branch of tree which hung overhead teetered a big black bird. The sun did not make its feathers look shiny and bright, but dull and dusty. Even its feet and bill were black, but, as it turned its head to one side and looked down at her, its eye glinted red. Sara disliked it on sight.

"Kaaaw—" It spread wide its wings, and, after a few vigorous flaps, took to the air, diving

at her head. Sara ducked as it circled her, its
hoarse cries sounding like jeering laughter.

Sara ran back under the tree, hoping the thick
branches would keep the bird off. But it settled
on a limb above her, walking along the bark and
watching her all the while.

"Go away!" Sara waved her arm.

"Kaaaw—" The bird jeered and flapped its
wings, opening its bill to a wide extent, ending
its cry with a hiss which was truly frightening.

Sara, holding to the basket, began to run. Once again the bird took off into the air and streaked down at her head. She jumped for the shelter of a bush, caught her foot on a root, and sprawled forward, scraping her knee painfully.

"Kaaaw—"

This time there was a different note in that sound, the jeer was gone. Sara sat up, nursing her skinned knee. The bush met in a green canopy over her head, and she could not see the bird, though she heard its cries plain enough.

Pattering into sight was the large fox she had met by the gate. With his attention fixed upon some point well above her head, he was snarling ferociously.

Mountain Road

Greg stood shivering in the middle of the moonlit road. He glanced back. Behind him was a dark valley, with no sign of the mirror through which he had come. A wind blew through the branches of the misshapen trees, finding a few leaves to move. It was a cold wind when it pushed against Greg. He hunched his shoulders against it and began to walk forward.

The road was not often used, he judged. In some places it was almost hidden by drifts of soil and in others the stone blocks of its surface were tilted up or down, with dried grass bunched in the cracks between them.

Now the road climbed, curving about the side of the rise. When Greg reached the top, he turned once more to look back. Only the road, running across a wasteland, was to be seen. No sign of any house or castle, nor could he sight any shelter ahead.

His legs began to ache with the strain of the steep climb. Now and again he sat down on one of the boulders brought down in old landslides. But while he rested he could hear nothing save the moan of the wind.

There were no more trees here, only small, thorny bushes without leaves, which Greg avoided after one bad scratch. He was sucking his hand when he heard a faint howl with a dim echo, coming from some place far ahead.

Three times that chilling cry sounded. Greg shivered. Wolf? He swallowed and strained to catch the last echo of that wail.

Now he looked down at the fork he was carrying, wondering what sort of defense that small weapon could be against a wolf attack. As he held it in the moonlight, testing the sharpness of the tines with his thumb, it glittered as had the dwarf-made blade Huon carried.

"Iron, cold iron." He repeated the words aloud without knowing just why. "Cold iron to arm me."

Greg stood up. Again he did not know why he must do this, but he tossed the fork from one hand to the other, and each time he caught it anew it was heavier, longer, sharper, until at last he was holding a four-foot shaft ending in four wickedly sharp points. Maybe this was another of Merlin's spells. It was a queer-looking spear but one which, added to the thought of Merlin, gave Greg confidence in spite of that distant howling.

The road was more and more broken. Sometimes the blocks were so disturbed Greg seemed to be climbing the steps of a stairway. And twice he edged about falls of earth, digging the fork-spear into the ground as support and anchor.

The moonlight, which had been so fresh and bright, was beginning to wane. Greg, seeing how bad the footing was here, and disliking the growing pools of shadow about, decided to camp until morning. He crawled into a hollow between two boulders and put his spear pointing out to seal the entrance.

He awoke stiff and cramped, so cramped that it hurt to move as he wriggled out of his half cave. It must be day but there was no sun. The world was gray, cloudy, but lighter than night. Greg found the trickle of a spring and sucked water from the palm of his hand, taking care to eat bites of his own food with the drink.

The road appeared to lead nowhere except up and up. There were no tracks in the patches of earth covering it, no trace that anyone save himself had been foolish enough to go that way for years. But, though no sun rose, the gray continued to lighten. Greg topped a narrow pass between two huge pillars of rock and gazed down into the cup of a valley, where a river ran fast under a humpbacked bridge. About that bridge, on both sides of the stream, were clusters of stone cottages, patches of green growing about them.

With a cry Greg hurried forward, half sliding down one slope, running down the next in his haste to reach the village and to see another person again.

"Halloooo!" He cupped his hands about his mouth, called out with all the force of his lungs.

The sound rolled about the valley, magnified and bounced back at him from the mountain walls. But there was no answer, no stir on the crooked street of the village. Alarmed now, Greg slowed his headlong pace, bringing his spear before him as he had the night before when he had taken refuge in the cave. He studied the huddle of dwellings with greater care. Most of them were small stone huts with thatched roofs. But now he could see that the thatch was missing in ragged patches, so that some of the houses were almost roofless.

However, just on the other side of the bridge, standing apart from the smaller buildings, was a square tower three stories high, with narrow slits of windows. And this did not seem so weatherworn.

Although Greg decided that the village had been long deserted, he was still alert. The green spots about the tumble-down cottages were rank with huge weeds with fat, unpleasant-looking leaves and small, dull purple flowers which gave out a sickly scent.

He hesitated on the bridge and then glanced quickly at the nearest cottage. The doorless entrance gaped like a toothless mouth, the window spaces were eyeholes lacking eyes. Yet Greg could not rid himself of the feeling that he was being spied upon, that someone or something was peering from that doorway, or from one of the windows, slyly—secretly—

As he moved, his spear struck against the stone parapet of the bridge with a clank of metal. And that sound, small as it was, was picked up, echoed through the empty village. Greg knew in that moment that he should never have shouted from the ridge, that perhaps he had drawn attention to himself in a manner he would regret.

Better to get out of the valley as quickly as he could. He tried to keep all those cottages in sight, sure that, if he were lucky, or fast, or clever enough, he would sooner or later catch a glimpse of what must lurk there.

Crossing the bridge, Greg came out on a stretch of moss-greened pavement about the base of the tower. As he drew level with the door, his spear turned in his hands in spite of the firm grip with which he held it, hurting his skin with the force of the movement. Alarmed, he stumbled forward a step or two, drawn against the wall toward the interior of the tower by some force that seemed to guide his spear.

Then he discovered he would either have to abandon his weapon or continue on inside. And since he dared not leave the spear behind, Greg advanced reluctantly, the odd weapon light and free in his hold as long as he followed its direction.

Within the tower the light was dim, for it came only through narrow slits of windows. All the lower story was one square room, empty except for powdery drifts of old leaves. Against the far wall was a stairway leading to a hole in the ceiling. This Greg mounted warily one step at a time, still urged along by the spear.

At last he reached the third and top room, which was as bare as the other two had been, and he was completely bewildered. There were three windows here, one in each of the three walls at his sides and back. In the wall fronting him there was the outline of a fourth window which had been bricked up, as had the gate through which they had come to Avalon.

Moved by the power against which he no longer struggled, Greg went to the fourth wall and pried at the sealing stones with his pronged spear. The mortar which had bound the stones must have been very weak, for at the first slight push they gave way, falling outward one after another.

Greg swung around to face the stairwell, sure that if any enemy lurked in the village the crash of the falling stones would bring him—or it—into the open.

But the echoes of the crash faded and there

was no other sound. Was the blocked window another gate? But it couldn't be—there was only sky to be seen without.

Greg put his hand on the wide sill and pulled himself up for a better view. The ruinous state of the village was even more apparent from this height. There was not a whole roof on any of the cottages, no signs of cultivation in the old fields beyond.

The puzzle of why he had been brought here— for Greg was certain he had been guided—was still a mystery. He studied the ground below and saw a ragged bush tremble where there was no wind, as if something crept beneath its masking.

From the village he looked to the far wall of the next mountain. The cloudiness of the day made it difficult to locate any landmarks ahead. Then Greg gripped his fork-spear tighter, for there was something—a pinprick of light far up, far beyond—a light which flickered as though it came from the leaping flames of a distant fire.

He realized that that distant gleam could not be sighted from any other point in the valley than where he now stood. And so it was easy to understand that that light was what he had been brought here to see, that it must be the mysterious goal of his journey.

And now as Greg went downstairs and out into the open, his spear did not resist his going. Only three houses stood between him and the open country, and he was eager to be away from the dead village. However, that was not yet done, as he discovered when he rounded the last hut.

Between him and the first scrubby growth of trees masking the upward slope of the road were what had once been fields. When he had inspected these from the tower, they had appeared to be only weedgrown spaces bordered by the rotting remains of ancient fences. And between them the road ran straight, walled by borders of half-dead hedges.

Greg halted and lowered the fork. For, flowing out of the hedgerows now, was a company of animals. They moved silently, every head swung so that eyes, yellow and green and red, were on him. Wolves—certainly the larger shapes of silver-gray were wolves—minks, weasels—all hunters, all gray of coat.

They stood in a dead tangle of grass, their heads showing above it, the bolder creatures crouched at the verge of the road. But they did not advance any farther. The wolves sat on their haunches as if they were hounds, their pink tongues showing a little. Greg gained confidence. Step by wary step he passed along the lane they had left open for him.

He watched those beads of eyes move as he moved, he held his breath as he stepped between the two wolves. Not daring to quicken pace lest he provoke them into attack, he kept on walking slowly through that strange company. But when he had reached the edge of the wood and dared to look back, the fields were as barren of life as they had been earlier. Whatever had been the purpose of that queer assembly, it had not meant danger for him.

Tired and hungry though he was, Greg began to climb again. He disliked that valley so much he did not want to pause again until he was safely out of it. But soon he ran into thickets of ripe berries and clipped them off in juicy handfuls, munching dry bits of sandwich between.

He spent that night in a rough lean-to he made by stacking branches together. And he slept soundly, though with troubled dreams. Then he awoke to another gray day.

Before he had gone a quarter mile the road forked. The wider, paved way he had followed since he had come through Merlin's mirror angled to the left. Another path, far less well marked and beginning with a very steep climb, went on ahead. And it was the latter which pointed in the direction of the spark he had sighted from the tower.

Greg studied the path. Up and up it angled, ending in the dark mouth of a deep cleft or cave. Again the fork-spear in his hands urged him up and into the very heart of that black opening. He tried to find a path around, but there was no possible one and the pull of the fork would not let him turn aside—unless he dropped it.

Greg crept forward and chill stone walls closed in on him far too quickly. Somewhere ahead he could hear the distant lap of water. He began to sound his way, rapping the fork against the rock flooring lest he fall into some underground stream.

The dark was so thick Greg had a queer feeling he could gather up its substance in his hands, hold it. When he glanced back, the entrance was a tiny glimmer of gray, so he could hardly distinguish it—then the passage climbed and there was only the terrifying dark, a dark which swallowed you up. He felt as if he could not breathe, that he was trapped. His heart pounded heavily. He wanted nothing so much as to turn and run and run—

Now he was listening, listening for all the things his imagination told him might lie in wait here. But somehow he kept going, his head swimming with the effort that determination cost him, not daring to pause lest he *would* hear something indeed.

"Iron, cold iron." First he whispered those words and then said them aloud in a kind of chant. And the fork-spear swung in time to that. The feel of it in his hands began to give him confidence—until at last he saw another gleam of gray light and came out on a ledge a few feet above a wide plateau down to which he could easily leap.

At the far side of the level plateau was a paved surface, and Greg saw that it was a sort of road that wound about a series of strange pillars. At first Greg thought they might be columns of a ruined building. Then he saw that they were clustered in irregular groups or scattered singly with no plan.

In the midst of these was the remains of a fire. The huge logs which had been piled to burn there were full tree trunks, and to transport them to this barren waste must have taken a great deal of labor. But he could see no carts, no men, though the fire was not quite dead. A thin trickle of smoke still curled, and the bitter tang of it hung in the air.

Greg dropped to the plateau and walked among the pillars toward the fire. Somehow, deep inside him, he knew that this was the goal of his journey and that he was now about to do what he had been sent to accomplish. That he was to recover one of the talismans, he did not doubt. Which treasure it was and whom he was to take it from still remained mysteries.

He was one pillar away from the fire when he put his hand against the last column. But there was no rock under his fingers—he touched something else! Greg snatched his hand away. Somewhere behind or above him he heard a chime as if a cord of silver bells had been shaken with warning vigor.

Sea Road

Sand moved under Eric's feet. And a sea bird screamed as it swooped to snatch a wriggling silver fish from the waves. Wind which was crisp and fresh blew against his face and pulled at Eric's hair.

He climbed to the top of the tallest dune to view the scene. The beach was wide. Behind the dune it rippled back to a point where dark patches might mark trees and bushes, but too far away for Eric to be sure. However, he was certain that his path, which was not a real one such as Greg had followed, lay seaward across the water.

So he faced in that direction, to sight a dark blot bobbing up and down, being brought to land by the breaking combers. A boat? Perhaps, though he could not be sure at this distance.

Farther out there was a smudge of shadow on the horizon. Since it did not move and was darker than any cloud, Eric thought it might be land, maybe an island. And because it lay directly ahead of the point where he had entered this country, he was sure that it was his goal.

No one could possibly expect him to *swim* way out there! Could he make it by boat—a good, steady boat?

Eric coasted down the seward side of the dune and trotted on to the damp sand where the waves broke. Slowly he pulled off his shirt and jeans and waded out. The water was cool, stinging where the briers had made scratches on his legs and arms. Before him, just out of reach, the boat drifted. Eric took another step or two and the footing dropped sharply away from beneath him. He splashed in over his head with a cry, threshed out wildly. He was right—water could never be trusted—try that and you were lost! Then a remnant of Slim's patient drilling at the camp swimming lessons last year returned to him and he floundered as far as the boat. Steadying himself with a hand on the gunwale, Eric looked the craft over. It was half full of water, which made it ride low, but there appeared to be no break in its sides and he thought if he could tow or push it ashore he could inspect it carefully and make sure.

That was easier to plan than to do. The boat was unhandy and sluggish, and Eric had to exert a great deal of effort to get it ashore. As its blunt bow thrust into the sand, he collapsed quite worn out.

He stumbled up after a while and rubbed himself dry on his shirt. More than anything else he wanted to stretch out and sleep, but the boat was waiting there and he had a queer feeling that time was important and he had none to waste.

Luckily it was a small boat and the material it was made of was very light so he could handle it alone. Upon closer examination Eric discovered that what covered its curved ribs was scaled skin. A giant fish might have been skinned to cover it.

Once the water was spilled out, the craft was buoyant and he pulled it all the way out of the water. Turned upside down so he could look for any breaks in its hull, it resembled a huge turtle with head, tail, and legs tucked into the shell. Dried by the sun the scales had a rainbow sheen, but they were as harsh as a file when Eric ran his hand across the surface.

Sure that it was intact, Eric sat down in the sand and ate a little of the food Sara had given him. He was thirsty, but nowhere on the dunes could he hope to find fresh water to drink.

Then he put the food packet and the spoon into the boat and pushed it afloat before climbing in. The weight of his body sank it into the waves, but it was only at that moment he realized he had neither oars nor paddle.

He was about to go ashore again to search for a piece of driftwood which might serve that purpose when his foot touched the spoon and he picked it up.

"Cold iron," he said loud, not knowing why.

Then he watched, round eyed with amazement. From a teaspoon it grew swiftly to ladle size in his grasp, then larger, until he was holding an object, spoon-shaped still, but as big as a small spade. Magic, real magic, he thought with a small thrill of excitement.

Large though it now was, the spoon's weight could still be handled easily. Not without fear that it might shrink as suddenly as it had enlarged, Eric dipped it overside experimentally and, using it as a paddle, headed out to sea, his goal that offshore island.

Eric was not an experienced boatman, nor were the skin boat and the spoon the best equipment for such a voyage. But he dipped the improvised paddle with energy, and the temporary smoothness of the water surface was in his favor. As he drew away from the beach the sea birds gathered above him, screaming to one another, and continued to escort him out to sea.

Practice helped. His first clumsiness lessened and his speed picked up, though he had difficulty in keeping the boat headed in the right direction. And, if he paused to rest his arms and shoulders, the incoming waves bore him back, to lose the painfully won distance. To Eric, the impatient one of the Lowrys, the very slowness of his advance was an added trial, but he continued on.

Slowly the island rose higher out of the water. There appeared to be no shore beach there. Cliffs rose directly from the sea to afford no landing place to anyone but a bird. The flock of birds that had been following Eric's slow progress now flapped ahead of the cliffs and settled down there.

As he drew nearer, inch by weary inch, Eric saw that even if some scrap of beach did exist at the foot of those rock walls there would be no way from it to the heights above. However, there were openings in the cliffs themselves, vast caves into which the sea pushed exploring fingers. Painfully Eric paddled his light craft around the end of a rocky point, hoping to find on the seaward side some landing place.

He circled the entire island, which was a small one, without finding what he sought. Yet he was certain that he *must* land here. And until he did so, and accomplished the task which had been assigned him by the mirror—or by Merlin— there was no going back.

Underneath his outward impatience Eric possessed a core of stubbornness. It was this that now held him to his weary round of paddling, though his shoulders ached and his arms felt leaden. If there was no beach, then he must find another way in—perhaps through one of those gaping caves. He chose the largest and paddled toward it.

The curve of the roof was high above his head, and for about three boat lengths the daylight lasted to guide him in. Eric used all his small skill to keep directly in midchannel, well away from the ledges of rock from which trailed lengths of green weed. The smell of the sea was strong, but with it also came another odor, not as pleasant.

As the light grew dimmer the walls began to draw together, and Eric feared his choice had not been a good one. But still he sent the boat on, even when the ledges came within scraping distance. For he believed he could see a wider area ahead. So sure was he of this that he poled the boat for the last foot or so, pushing the spoon against the rocks for leverage. There was a scrape and then he floated into a lighted space.

Far overhead a break in the rock framed the sky, and the sun shot dusty rays to a pool of quiet water. To Eric's left was the beach he had sought, showing dry white sand well above the water line.

When the keel of the boat grated on the miniature beach, Eric crawled over the blunt bow, pulling the light craft up behind him. The smell of the sea was strong here, as it had been in the outer cave, but with it was that other odor.

Eric drew the boat entirely out of the water before he explored farther. There was no way of reaching that hole far above. But the beach sloped up, and since there was no back wall to be seen as yet he started to walk on it.

He was really thirsty now, his longing for a

drink increased by the sound of the sea's wash around the rocks. And he hoped to discover a spring or fresh-water pool on the surface of the island. The memory of the lemonade he had drunk so long ago made him run a parched tongue over his dry lips.

The beach slope continued upward, bringing him to a dark crevice. Eric hesitated. It was so dark in there and the thought of pushing on was not a happy one.

At last, extending the spoon before him to test the footing, he advanced. The crevice proved to be a short corridor, ending in a well. Only now, against the circle of free sky above, could he see the rough projections and hollows which provided holds for the hands and feet of a determined climber.

Fastening the spoon to his belt, Eric began to work his way up. Had it not been for his thirst he would not have found this a difficult venture. But now all he could think of was the need for fresh water—lots of water—and quickly found.

He made a last hard pull and was out, to lie panting on a mat of coarse grass. The cries of the sea birds were loud and shrill, their screams rising to a deafening din. And the odd smell which had hung in the cave was much stronger here. He sat up to look around.

The cliffs which were the sea wall of the island were, in fact, the outer sides of a giant bowl. By a series of ledges the land within descended to a valley, the center point of which could not be far above sea level.

Those ledges were covered by patches of rank green grass, but they also afforded lodging places for hundreds of nests—old nests, Eric decided, after examining the nearest. If this was the community nursery of the sea birds it was not in active use at present.

In the very center of the round valley was a vast mass of sticks and rubbish which might have been gathered by some giant among birds. Or did it mark where the refuse of years of nests had been brushed and wind-blown?

What interested Eric far more at the present was the sight of a small trickle of water splashing from ledge to ledge on the far side of the cup-shaped valley. He was sure such a tiny rivulet was not born of the sea, and it was what he wanted most at the moment.

He started around the valley, not wanting to take the more direct route over the odorous mass in the center. The birds continued to wheel and call about him, rising into the air as he passed, settling down on the ledge behind him.

They seemed, he thought once, rather like spectators gathering for a promised show. And he was sure that more and more of them were winging in from the sea to settle about the upper rim of the bowl. But none of them flew at him or tried to defend the old nests. And he did not fear their presence.

Only—there was such an attitude of waiting that Eric's uneasiness increased. He now noticed that though all the upper ledges were thick with nests the fresher masses of dried materials there were based on moldering remains of earlier building; yet, for a good space about the mass in the center, there were no smaller nests at all and the wide ledges were bare.

Eric made the journey to that thread of stream and drank from his cupped hands, taking a bite of bread with the welcome water. Then he splashed handfuls of it over his hot face and neck. From this point he had a good view of the stuff in the center of the dip. And the longer he studied it the stronger grew that unpleasant suspicion that it was not driftage from the old nests on the upper ledges but a huge nest in its own right, entwined and woven in its present state and size with purpose.

"For an eagle?" Eric wondered, wishing he knew more about birds. He remembered some pictures in an old *National Geographic* of a bird in South America—a condor. Yes, that was it— a condor! Those grew to be so large they could carry off a sheep. Was this the nest of a condor?

Judging by their condition, the other nests were all last season's; perhaps the same was true of the large one. Eric sat gazing down. The last thing he wanted to do was to descend and rake through that mess. Yet, just as he had been drawn to the island from the shore, so was he being drawn to that big nest.

He hunched forward, his elbows planted on his knees, his cupped hands supporting his chin. There were strange things caught in that tangle. He was sure that he had seen the glint of sun reflected from metal.

But the present odd behavior of the birds kept him from exploring. The upper ledges were now packed almost solid with them. And their cries and calls were dying away. They perched there, one folded wing against the next, all eying him. Eric did not like it. He wanted to retreat to the sea cave, to the boat waiting there. Only, he could not.

Then the spoon, which had been fastened to his belt, slipped free. Eric grabbed for it without success. It clattered down on one of the lower bare ledges, gave a bounce, and flew out into the very heart of the massive nest. There it stood, handle up, bowl buried deep.

He could not go back to the boat without it. Eric stood up. The birds were so quiet they all might have been holding their breath to watch some important action. Within him Eric feared that once he touched that giant nest he would provoke some unheard-of danger. He had to get the spoon and yet he dared not!

Fighting his fear Eric dropped from one ledge to the next, descending to the mass of withered sticks and other material. In order to reach the spoon he must jump out into the very center of the mess.

Now not a bird called, there was no sound at all in that queer valley. Eric jumped. From far off there came a shrill scream as he crashed down, waist-deep, in the stuff of the nest.

Woods Road

In the wood where Merlin's mirror had brought her, Sara pushed back into the shelter of the bush and watched the fox anxiously, not sure that he was friendly. But she was certain that his anger was for the bird hidden somewhere in the branches above her. She hoped that his coming would drive the vicious crow—or whatever it was—away. She could still hear the bird moving about. It no longer called, but the scrape of claws on bark, a rustle as if it fanned its wings, reached her.

The fox was now gazing straight at her. Meeting that intent regard, Sara was no longer frightened. She wriggled forward out of the bush and got up, brushing dirt and dead twigs from her shirt and jeans. There was a flutter in the tree

and the fox snarled menacingly. Then the bird
flew out well above them and circled.

"Kaaaw—" But it was a scream of anger and
defeat.

The fox answered with a sharp bark, and the
black bird soared, vanishing above the treetops.
Sara thankfully watched it go. Its harsh croaking
could be heard dying away in the distance, and
the girl sighed with relief. True, it had been only
a bird, but there was something in its attack upon
her which had been the more frightening because
it *was* a bird, a creature so much smaller than
herself, that had wanted to hurt her.

The gentlest of tugs at the bottom of her jeans
drew her attention from the treetops to her new
companion. The fox was mouhing the fabric as
might an affectionate dog, first pulling and then
trotting a few paces on, looking back in invitation.
Sara picked up the basket to follow.

The red tail with its pointed white tip waved
briskly from side to side as her guide led her
between two bushes and so into a path where the
saplings and undergrowth reached higher and
higher until they met in a green arch overhead.
They were not alone in this green world. Although
Sara saw no one but the fox, she could hear all
kinds of small squeakings, rustlings, and patter-
ings behind the leaf walls, as though a crowd of
small forest people were gathering to watch them
pass and talking in their own language.

The green road was growing dusky as light-leaved bushes gave way to dark-needled evergreens. And the pleasant, spicy odor, as well as the spring carpet of castoff needles underfoot, made the journey pleasant, in spite of the increasing shadows.

Now that they were among the evergreens, these sounds made by the unseen watchers died away, and the fox slowed his pace. His pointed ears pricked forward and, seeing his caution, Sara felt uneasy again. The darkness was full of menace and she pressed on until she felt the reassuring brush of the plumed tail against her legs.

For how long they followed the road, Sara could never afterward tell. She only knew that when they came to a clearing she was very tired and hungry, glad to sit down on a mat of pine needles and moss. The fox sat down also, his tongue lolling from his jaws.

"Are you hungry?" The three words sounded very loud in the dim place, making Sara sorry she had spoken. She opened the basket and took out a sandwich, carefully breaking it in half. The bread was beginning to dry and curl up at the edges and the peanut butter was all caked. Ordinarily she would have thrown it away, but now she ate it eagerly, offering the other half to the fox.

He eyed it curiously and then, slowly and unmistakably, he shook his head. Sara tried to eat slowly, making each bite last as long as possible.

But she could not deny that she was still hungry, even after picking up the last crumb.

The fox was on his feet again, plainly waiting for her. Then they could both hear, faint and far above, that "kaaaw." This time it came from more than one bird. The fox backed against Sara, forcing her by the pressure of his body into the shadows under the trees. His head was up as he gazed into the circle of sky above the clearing.

Sara saw a line of birds skimming across the open. They were high above the clearing and none of them appeared to notice the two standing there.

"Kaaaw—"

The last bird in line fell away and swooped down. The fox ushered Sara into a hollow between two trees. Once they were safely under cover, the fox turned his head to her. He was laughing in his own way and Sara managed a small answering smile. The more she saw of those black birds the less she liked them.

The trail brought them to a brook, but the fox would not let her approach the stream until he had prowled along the bank, pausing to listen and peer up into tree branches. If any of the black birds were hidden there to spy, they were cunning enough not to betray themselves. The fox went down to lap water and Sara joined him. But he was impatient, mouthing her sleeve in warning before she had had more than a few sips to drink.

They traveled across a fallen log bridge and

into the path on the other side. Then the fox came to an abrupt halt, one front paw slightly raised. Across the path, stretched in unbroken perfection, was a gauzy circle of spider web. It was the largest one Sara had ever seen and she stood very still, her heart beating fast. How large was the spider that would spin a web like that?

The fox whined softly as might a dog faced by some problem it could not solve. Plainly he did not want to touch the web. Hating the thing herself, Sara picked up a dried branch and thrust it at the lacy circle, expecting it to break into a few floating strands.

To her horror the branch bounced back. With more caution Sara brought the branch against one of the threads anchoring the web to the ground, with no better result. Delicate though the web seemed, it could not be so easily broken. And she could not bring herself to touch it with her bare hands.

They could not go around it, for here the bushes and trees so walled them in that they could not break through. Also, and this worried Sara most of all, how could they be sure that the spinner of that rubbery web was not lurking somewhere off the trail to meet them?

The web might be cut with a knife—if she had one. If she only had the fiery silver blade Huon wore! But what had he said—iron was poison to the creatures of Avalon? Iron . . . the steel knives in the picnic basket!

Sara took one out. It was a rather blunt-edged blade, made more for spreading than cutting. But maybe she could saw through the strand of web with it.

Twice only did the steel touch the web. Sara sat back on her heels with a cry of amazement. From the spot where she had tried to cut through, the threads were shriveling. In a matter of seconds the web was gone and the path open. The fox barked in approval and Sara flung her arms about his neck, hugging him while he politely touched his nose to her cheek.

She kept the knife ready in her hand, but they came upon no more of the elastic webs as they started to climb a gradual slope. Though the trees became smaller and fewer there were still many bushes and the fox kept close to these, pushing Sara into their shadows time and time again.

At last they were faced with a wide space where only grass grew. The fox barked twice and crouched low, wriggling forward a length or so, demonstrating caution to the girl. So, worm-fashion, hot and scraped, Sara was guided to the top of a small knoll from which the fox indicated they were to spy out the country ahead.

From the knoll the ground sank once again. Sara, seeing what lay in the hollow, could not help shuddering. There was a wood of trees. But they were all stark and dead, pointing leafless branches to the sky. Around the outer edge of the wood, bands of gray stuff reached from tree trunk to tree trunk, as if lengths of material had been tightly stretched into a wall reaching higher than Sara's head. And that gray stuff was spider webs, hundreds, millions of spider webs, woven one above the other into a thick blanket.

Where were the spinners of those choking strands? Sara tried hard not to think about what they must look like, how big they would be. Surely the fox did not mean for them to go in there! Only, inwardly, Sara was sure that was just why she had been brought to this place.

The knife had broken one web. But would it work as well against that wall binding the whole dead forest? And if she did cut a path for them would they then be faced by some kind of creatures who *liked* to live in a dead wood protected by a spider-web wall? For that wall must have been fashioned to protect or imprison *something,* something Sara did not wish in the least to meet.

However, the fox did not urge her forward to attack the sticky wall. Instead he retreated, working his way back to the wood from which they had come. When they were once more in the cover of the forest, the fox lay down, his head resting on his outstretched fore-paws. He closed his eyes slowly and then opened them.

They were to stay there and rest, she translated. A nest of dried leaves against a fallen tree trunk seemed very soft to her as she curled up in it. She was sure her companion would not allow either bird or spider near her, and she was very tired indeed.

Something soft, maybe the blanket, moved against her chin. . . . Sara opened her eyes. The fox stood over her, the paw with which he had roused her still raised. He whined very softly deep in his throat, and she took that as a warning, pulling out of the leaf nest with as little noise as possible.

It was close to sunset. The shadows under the trees had grown long. From the top of the fallen log the fox whined again. Sara climbed up beside him and on the ground ahead saw a strange sight.

The dark soil had been cleared of leaves and sticks. In the middle of the space sat the picnic basket, and ranged out from it were stones of all sizes and shapes laid out in the form of a star within a circle. At the five points of the star small piles of green leaves were heaped.

Again the fox whined and pushed against her. Sara walked forward until she stood beside the basket. As she looked back at the animal his head bobbed up and down in approval. She was doing as he wished.

Completely puzzled she waited, watching as he trotted purposefully from one small pile of leaves to the next. He shoved at each with a forepaw, having first nosed it. What he was doing, or why, she could not guess.

When he had completed his circle he sat down on his haunches and then reared up, holding his front paws into the air. As he barked and whined he moved his paws, and for some reason Sara found it necessary to sit down. No, not really to sit down, but to kneel, her hands on the ground as if she must copy the usual four-footed position of the fox.

Thin trails of mist rose from the leaf piles, though Sara was sure they were not afire, for she could see no flames. She smelled a wonderful spicy scent, like a combination of pine needles warmed by the sun and the cloves Mrs. Steiner used in cooking. The smoke from the little piles of leaves grew thicker and thicker, closing about her. Now Sara could not see the fox, nor anything outside the star and circle.

The smoke had made her head dizzy and queer. She wondered if she was dreaming all this, for everything looked so odd. A little frightened, she tried to get up. But her hands did not push properly—in fact, she no longer had hands!

Paws covered with gray fur rested on the ground. And there was the same gray fur up her arms! Sara swung her head about—gray fur all over her body—a gray tail behind her. Who—what was she?

Sara tried to scream. But the sound she made was very different indeed—

"Merrrow!" That was the wail of a terrified cat!

The smoke was lifting. She could see the star points, each marked by a cone of white ash where the leaves had been. And, as that curtain disappeared, she saw the fox, now looming well above her in a very disturbing way.

"Come!" The word might have been a bark to Sara-the-girl's hearing, but to Sara-the-cat it made sense. However, she remained where she was, letting the fox kick and paw inside some stones of the pattern to approach her, her protests and demands for explanation expressed in a series of yowls and hisses, while the hair stiffened along her humped spine and her tail lashed angrily.

"Come!" The fox stood over her. "The shape-changing does not last past tomorrow's dawn and there is much to do."

"What have you done to me?" Sara demanded. "I am not a cat!"

"That is true. But as a human you could not enter the Castle of the Wood. And that you must do, lest all of us of the woods and fields of Avalon be put to the service of the Dark Ones."

"How?"

"Did not Huon tell you of Wizard Merlin's ring? He who wears it upon his hand can shape and make animal and bird, tree and bush, either for good or ill. While Merlin wore it, it was used only for good—the good of all good things—the ill of all evil things. But now it has fallen into the hands of evil, so will its use be wholly to the ill of all. But evil does not yet dare to use it openly. So it has been hidden away in the Castle of the Wood, where only one armed with cold iron and the magic of cold iron may enter to bring it forth. Since evil knows at once when a human approaches its secret places, you must put on the guise of one of us. The shape you now wear will last until the rising of tomorrow's sun. So you must hurry, taking with you that iron which is your own magic."

He nosed the basket open and pointed to the knife Sara had used against the web. Bracing her paws against the edge of the basket, Sara pulled it from the webbing. It was an awkward thing to carry in her mouth as now she must.

Her earlier fright and anger were ebbing. Somehow the longer she wore the cat body the more natural it seemed. And this was going to be an exciting adventure. She was eager to be off.

The fox gave a last warning. "You must return here, to this place, and enter into the circle and star before you change, lest you be given another shape which is not of my choosing. If evil flows behind you, it cannot follow here. Be on your way now, gray sister!"

Sara skimmed up the hillock once more. She found she could run without a sound and that her new body was good for such sly work. It was already dusk in the vale, and in that gloom the spider-web walls had a soft glow of their own.

The Sword

In the stone wasteland of the mountains Greg felt so alone. As the chime of the bells sounded he stood very still, his head up, looking about. The stretch of mountain wall was far away and none of the strange pillars were crowned with belfries. Some thin and lazy wisps of smoke rose from the charred logs of the fire, but there was nothing else to be seen.

The pillars! While the bells still clamored, Greg returned to the pillar he had leaned against. To the eye it was a tall, rough, column of stone. Yet to the touch it was far different.

Once more Greg put out his hand, and the tips of his fingers moved not over stone but over the smoothness of metal and the soft texture of leather. For the second time he jerked away from that contact. Why should stone feel like a body dressed in scaly armor and leather? Why did his eyes tell him one thing, and his fingers another?

"Is—is there anyone here?" He meant that call to be louder than the bells, but it came from his lips hardly above a whisper. The rock pillar remained a rock to his eyes. Nothing moved. But now the sound of the bell, instead of chiming from all parts of the plateau, centered on one point across the dying fire. And more smoke puffed from the ashy brands, although no more wood had been added.

"Who is there?" Greg called again.

"There is no need to shout, sir squire."

Greg gaped. One moment the space across the fire had been empty, now someone stood there. For a second he thought it Merlin, for the person wore the same long gray robe he had seen on the wizard. Then, perhaps because his fears made him more alert, Greg knew the difference. Merlin's gray had been patterned with threads of red and it had been a silver-gray, the color of a sword blade.

But this newcomer was cloaked, and hooded as well, in the dull gray of winter storm clouds, and the patterns were in black thread, as was the girdle. Greg had felt awe for Merlin, but this stranger aroused fear. And instinctively Greg raised his fork-spear with the tines pointing to the other.

The stranger laughed gaily. White hands threw

back the hood and a woman faced Greg. Her hair tumbled out of the sack of the hood and fell about her shoulders, its ends reaching below her girdle. The locks were not dark, not fair, but the color of the silver blade Huon had shown them. And they appeared to throw off sparks of glittering light, as the dagger had drawn and reflected the sunlight.

She gathered up a handful of hair and spread it wide across her palm, then broke loose one, two, three of the long hairs. And, as she stood smiling at him, she rolled these together between thumb and forefinger.

"Why do you come here, sir squire?" she asked softly. "Also, it would seem that you do not like the open road, since you crept upon me by a back way." Her tone was that of an adult reproving a naughty child. But it was a tone Greg had heard many times in the past and it did not shame him. In that the witch made her first mistake, for he was not thrown off guard in confusion.

"I came by the road shown me," Greg answered, not knowing just why he chose those particular words, but knowing that they did not please the witch.

"Oh, and who guided you on that road?" It was a sharp demand.

Again Greg found words which were strange to him. "That which shines across stone—stone of body—stone of mind—"

"So! You are of those, are you!" Her eyes blazed green at him and her fingers moved very fast, weaving the cord she had spun of her three hairs into a net. "Then join your fellows!"

She cast the net at him over the charred logs and it expanded in the air as if to engulf his whole body. Greg thrust at it with the spear. The tines tangled in the mesh, wrapping it about the spear. One strand whipped about Greg's hand and wrist, clinging tightly.

But in seconds those strands which had caught on the prongs lost their silvery gleam, blackened, withered away to threads, and fell harmlessly to the ground. The bells shrilled in a wild clamor and the woman retreated a step or two, her clenched hand at her mouth, staring at him.

"Iron—a master of iron!" she half wailed. "Who are you who dares bring cold iron into the Stone Waste and takes no harm from it? Whom do you serve?"

"Merlin sent me."

"Merlin!" she spat the name in a snake's hiss. "Merlin, who is between the worlds so he can touch iron, and that silly boy Huon, who was born a mortal so he can wield iron as a sword, wear it as a shield, and that Arthur, a stupid, roaring bully of a king, who brought iron with him into Avalon—to poison those greater than he dared dream of being! May they rot and perish, may iron turn against them and sear the flesh from their crooked bones, may they be eaten up by the demons of the night! And you," she stared at Greg, "you are not Merlin, though he is a master at shape changing. But with his ring gone from his hand"—she laughed harshly—"he could not put on any disguise which would hide him from me. And you are not Huon, and certainly not Arthur! So I command you, boy, tell me your true name?" She was smiling and her voice had grown soft again.

"Gregory Lowry," he replied, in spite of himself.

But that answer did not appear to please her in the least. She repeated the name, her hands moving in complicated gestures as they had done when she had woven the net of hair. Then she threw them up in a movement expressing impatience and defeat.

"You hold iron, against that I may not set any spell. Well, what do you want of me?"

"That which is hidden." For the third time Greg spoke words someone, or something, else had put in his mouth.

She laughed loudly. "That you shall not have! Look about you, rash child. Where will you find that which is hidden? If you search here for forty days and forty nights, still will it remain safe for me!"

The pronged spear moved in Greg's hold, as it had moved to draw him into the tower in the deserted village. Slowly the points reversed, heading earthward. Greg had a flash of memory—

people hunting water with a forked stick which turned to the ground where a well might be dug —he had read about that. Could the fork-spear guide him to what must be found? He would try.

But he did not have to move far in his quest, for the weapon nearly flipped out of his grasp as he approached the fire, thrusting the tine tips into the mass of burnt wood and ash. Greg, kicking aside charred ends, began to dig.

The bells were no longer silver chimes, they were a harsh clamor beating in his ears, making him deaf and dizzy with their din. And the witch sped around and around the fire, though she prudently kept beyond spear reach, shouting strange words and making those patterns in the air with her hands.

A fearsome scaled thing, neither snake nor crocodile but a nasty mixture of both, squatted near, reached out claws to menace him. Greg swung the spear, brushed those claws, and the thing was gone. Other horrors gathered to ring him in, but Greg, feeling secure in the power of iron, did not even try to get rid of them. He continued to fork away earth from where the fire had burned.

It was slow work, for the fork did not serve well as a shovel and he was afraid to put it down and use his hands. In the end he squatted, holding the fork with one hand and shoveling out the loosened soil with the other. Then his groping fingers found something to tug at—

The object came up and it was so heavy he had difficulty in shaking it free of the dirt. But what he held was a sword!

Greg had seen its like in a museum and he had wondered then how any man had had strength enough to swing it. For its broad blade and heavy cross hilt weighed down hand and arm. A sword—the missing talisman—Excalibur!

He put the spear between his knees for safe-keeping and brushed the clay dust from the hilt and glimmering blade of the sword. It was very plain, bearing no bright gems, no wealth of gold, but he was sure this was what he had been sent to discover. Greg held it tight to him in his left arm as he looked up at the witch.

She no longer strove to weave spells, but stood quietly, eying him narrowly in return. And, as he backed away from the hole, Greg had the feeling that while she had lost the sword, she still believed that she had a chance for victory. Was it chance, or some more of Merlin's long-distance magic that had solved part of her secret for him?

For, as he backed away, the tip of the sword struck hard against one of the pillars. And that blow was answered by a choked cry!

Where the pillar had been stood a man, or rather swayed a man, his eyes closed, his face very white. He wore armor and leather like Huon's elf knights, but his surcoat was white with a red dragon for its device. He moaned and his eyes opened.

" 'Ware the witch!"

A net of hair whirled through the air. Greg caught it on his spear before it could touch the man and it withered away.

The witch screamed and the sound was not a human cry. In her place, a huge gray bird fluttered wings in rage and ran at Greg with cruel curved beak wide open. The boy swung the spear and the creature dodged, scurried on for a few feet, and took to the air, disappearing over the mountain. Then there was utter silence, for even the bells had ceased to chime.

"The sword!"

The man who had been a pillar was on his knees, his eyes wide and happy as they rested on the blade Greg held. "Sir, I beg of you, free this company. And then let us ride fast and hard. For Arthur's sword must rest in Arthur's hand before the enemy strikes into the very heart of Avalon! Time is passing very fast."

One by one Greg touched the pillars on the plateau and then the larger boulders which lay among them, until a company of men wearing the badge of the Red Dragon and their horses were living creatures once again. They left, two of the guardsmen riding double so that Greg might have a mount to himself.

The road was too broken to allow them a fast ride, but the knight Greg had first freed kept them to the best pace they could. They rounded the mountainside to the meeting of the cliff road, and before them now was the valley of the deserted village. It was close to sundown and Greg's dread of spending the night in that haunted place grew with every horse length they advanced. He tried to argue his companions into a night halt where they were, but to that they would not agree.

"You do not understand, youth. Now that the sword is out of their hands, they dare no longer hesitate in the attack. They must move before we reach Arthur or fail—and they still have the horn and the ring to hold against us. Thus if they can strike before we return Excalibur to the king, they will have some chance of victory, since only he dares carry the blade into battle. We must ride by night and day lest that chance be proven true."

"Huon's horses are winged. If we had those—" Greg said.

"The Warden of the West is served by the Horses of the Hills. But those are few in number and answer only the call of the Green Dragon, not the Red. Most strongly do I also wish they were with us at this hour!"

Greg could see the buildings of the village now, the tower, the humpbacked bridge. They had ridden to the edge of the fields where the road ran between hedgerows and he had walked through the lines of animals. What had been the purpose of that gathering? Where now were the wolves, all the rest?

He did not see the thing that scuttled out of

the bushes. Greg's first awareness of danger came when the horse he was riding reared high and he was nearly spilled from the saddle. Greg was no horseman and it was all he could do to cling to the saddle horn with one hand and the precious sword with the other, while his fork-spear fell to the ground.

That which had halted in the road before his mount had been no larger than a small dog, but it was growing fast into a scaled thing such as the witch had summoned on the plateau. Its taloned forepaw arched up above mount and rider, then flashed down.

Greg let go his hold on the saddle horn. With both hands he raised the sword; it was far too heavy for him to swing. The paw of the other came down, was impaled. The creature screamed and tried to jerk back; Greg was torn from the saddle. As he fell, in spite of his efforts, he lost his grip on the sword. Defenseless he faced the full fury of the giant dragon-thing.

The horse bolted, scattering the men who were fighting the frenzied fear of their own mounts. Greg saw the knight who led them trying to reach him.

Excalibur! Where was the sword? It had fallen from the thing's paw and lay in the road dust between Greg and the monster. The wounded limb of the reptile was shrunken and powerless, and perhaps the blade between Greg and the dragon prevented a second attack. Greg tried to look for his spear and watch the monster at the same time. Suddenly a gray shadow leaped from the hedge and slashed at the scaled tail, and Greg heard the howled challenge of a wolf. As the spined head of the thing flashed around to this new annoyance, Greg caught up his spear.

A second wolf howl rent the air, but it was a cry of anger and not of fear. Up over the road rose a wave of animals, large and small, all heading for the dragon-thing, their teeth gleaming as they came. The monster stamped its feet, swept with its tail, shrilled red rage.

Then it leaped high, springing over the sword, looming above Greg. But excited though it was, the dragon flinched from the spear prongs. Greg lunged and the monster gave way, making a fatal mistake, for on its second retreat the bulk of its underbody came down on the sword.

Its head cracked skyward and it bellowed, twisting back and forth, but seemingly unable to move from that spot, as if the blade upon which it now crouched was a trap. The outlines of its body wavered, grew smaller. Greg saw that it was no longer a dragon but the gray-robed witch of the plateau. She shivered and shuddered, but her two feet were locked to the blade of Excalibur and there she was held fast.

On her robe the black lines rippled and ran, her silver hair writhed about her as if every strand had a life of its own. Then there was a flash and the woman was gone. A column of smoke wavered, sinking lower and lower. Save for the sword the road was now empty.

But only for the moment. From the hedges and fields there were rustlings, the sounds of many voices crying out in surprise and thanksgiving. Where the animals had swarmed to help in Greg's battle now moved men and women who stared dazedly at their own hands and feet, felt their bodies, looked at each other in amazement and joy.

The knight, his horse once again under control, came pounding up. On his face there was a wild elation.

"The Witch of the Mountains is naught!" he shouted. "Behold the ruler of the Stone Waste is gone from Avalon and with her dies the evil she has done! One of the enemy is vanquished. Rejoice you people, freed from the spell of the night."

The Horn

On the sea island Eric stood with his feet deeply buried in the mass of dried stuff which formed the huge nest. He had to flounder a step or two farther to lay hands on the spoon. And it was tough wading, for his weight broke through the brittle stuff easily and gave him no steady footing. All he wanted to do was retrieve the spoon and get back to the safety of the ledges.

But Eric could not help noticing that there were odd things caught in the material of the untidy nest. A chain of gold was laced back and forth in a bundle of dried grass. Near it was a piece of tattered and faded cloth still bearing an embroidered device.

He had hold of the spoon now and tried to work it free of the sticks. But its bowl seemed to be so wedged into a hollow that he could not pull it loose. At last he was forced to tear at the mass with his hands, throwing aside wads of grass and broken branches.

It was very hot in the cup-shaped valley under the full rays of the sun and Eric paused now and again to rub his sleeve across his sweating face. The dust and grit he had stirred up in his job of destruction powdered his sweaty skin, got in his eyes and mouth. But he worked on, determined to free the spoon.

At first he thought there was a cloud lowering overhead when a shadow crossed the nest. But a sense of danger warned him and he looked up, only to cower frantically down into the wreckage he had made.

Earlier he had tried to imagine what kind of bird had built that nest. Now he knew. But to see it alive was worse than to picture it in his mind. And could that monster be only a bird? For what kind of bird had a scaled rather than a feathered head? Yet it did have feathers, black feathers, on its body, and those giant wings which flapped in thunderclaps of sound as it circled the island were fashioned like a bird's, if on a huge scale.

Eric dug at the mass of nest under him, hoping to burrow into hiding until the bird was gone. For he was very sure if he attempted to reach the open ledges he would be exposing himself to instant attack. That scaled head was armed with the curved beak of a hunter, and the feet, drawn up to its body as it flew, were taloned.

He was holding to the spoon, and at last at his frantic tug it loosened, uprooting a vast heap of the nest material. Eric threw himself into that evil-smelling hollow. The original foundation of the huge nest had been laid across a depression. As he jumped, this foundation splintered, disclosing a small cleft in the rock floor beneath. Eric poked the spoon into this, having no wish to fall to the sea caves below. But the metal rang on rock, finding a bottom to the crevice a few feet down.

A screech from overhead—a shriek such as a diving jet might have made—set Eric to pushing and squeezing into the hole, raking his shoulders, tearing his shirt. But he was safely flattened in the rock-walled crevice when the bird-thing landed, defeaning him with wild squawks.

It was the very fury of the bird which saved Eric. For it tore at the nest, and the mass of stuff it dislodged fell across the hole, covering him. He lay there, his mouth dry, his hands shaking on the handle of the spoon. Shivering, he waited for the covering to be scratched aside, and claw or beak to pluck him out. Once a talon scraped across the rock surface just above him. But the crevice saved him from discovery.

Only, how long could he stay there? The loose stuff was being torn and tossed about, so a

measure of air reached him. But that was limited.
And if he moved he would be seen.

With his hands Eric began to explore the narrow space in which he lay. Its width was hardly
more than that of his shoulders, but it was longer
than he was tall. Deeper, too, than he had first
thought, for small trash from the nest had sifted
into it. He was pressed down upon small branches,
powdery vegetation which smelled of decay.

Eric began to dig this from under him. From
sounds he could tell that the bird was still searching for him, but in such a mindless way that Eric
began to believe it was a stupid creature. If that
dim wit led to its forgetting him quickly, he had a
good chance at escape.

Meanwhile he cleared a passage along the
crevice, pushing the loose trash behind him with
his feet. Then his head bumped an obstruction
not so easily moved. Eric explored by touch, dis-
covering this was no branch, for he fingered the
smoothness of metal which curved sleekly.

When he tugged, the object yielded, but also
he brought disaster on himself, for the whole
brush heap heaved. And the bird could not have
been as stupid as Eric hoped, as there was an
answering flurry above. Eric gasped and choked
as dust filled his mouth and blinded his eyes.

Then the whole mass over him was raked away.
Eric blinked watering eyes up at the bird head
curving down to him, the beak open. Fortunately
the head had to turn to one side before it was in

striking range. Eric swung up the spoon in a last wild try at defense.

That beak struck the metal bowl with enough force to smash it back against Eric's body, driving most of the air out of his cramped lungs. He lay scarlet-faced and gasping, waiting numbly for a second blow.

When that did not come he edged about, trying to rise from the crevice. Though his eyes smarted from the dust, he could see more clearly now—until a violent flapping of the wings stirred the litter into a murky storm cloud.

The bird, its wings beating frantically, was shaking its head from side to side. And there was something odd about that head, too, though the creature's jerky movements kept Eric from a close examination. He got to his feet, the spoon held up before him.

A second time the head darted down. Eric, with all the energy he could summon, swung the spoon as he might a bat. The improvised club met the head squarely with an impact which crumpled Eric to his knees. Then the wings beat, lifting the creature into the air above the bowl. It made no sound and its head bobbed limply on its breast. Up and up it climbed and Eric stood to watch it. Was it going to strike at him from that height? Only the loosely dangling head, the now faltering beat of the wings, made him hope he had had the better of their meeting.

The birds were rising from the ledges to join

the creature. But not for long did they escort it. The great wings clapped for the last time, closed against the half-feathered, half-scaled body, and the thing fell toward the sea. That it was dead, or at least mortally wounded, Eric no longer doubted.

Keeping the spoon in the crook of his arm for safety, he wiped the dust and dirt from his face. He was not sure yet just how it had happened, or why the bird had died. What Huon had told them of iron being poison to those of Avalon must be true. And he was grateful for that.

The walls of the crevice, uncovered for a good length by the bird's last efforts, were waist-high about him and Eric started to climb out, eager to reach the spring on the ledge and rinse the dust from his mouth and throat. But there was something looped about his ankle and he stooped to free it.

He was holding a strap of leather, old, but well oiled and still limber, and it had small gold stars and symbols he did not understand set into it. It could not have been hidden there long. When he pulled he discovered it was anchored to something still wedged in the wreckage of the nest.

Eric scooped away the sticks with the spoon handle. Metal gleamed up at him, not gold this time but silver, banding a duller white. He had uncovered a horn of ivory and silver.

Shaking it free, Eric held his find up to the light of day. It could not have lain long in concealment for the silver was not tarnished. A horn! Huon's horn! He had found one of the lost talismans.

Tempted, Eric rubbed the mouthpiece on his sleeve and put it to his lips. But he did not blow. There was something about the horn which was not of the world he knew. Telling himself that a call might bring another of the giant birds, Eric slung the strap over his shoulder and clawed his way back through the debris to the ledge spring where he drank deeply and ate of his food packet.

How long he had been on that island he could not have told. And time in Avalon and his own world ran differently—had not Merlin said something like that? It seemed as if he had been there for hours, yet just now it was drawing close to sunset.

Dared he try the trip back to shore by night? Eager as he was to be away from the nesting place, Eric was reluctant to set forth from the island. There was too much chance of being carried seaward in the boat. And he was too tired to paddle back. Every bone in his body ached with weariness.

Where *could* he spend the coming night? Eric shrank from the destroyed nest and the ledges about it. Better return to the sea cave and sleep in the boat, fearful though he had always been of water. And he had also better climb back before night.

Eric began the descent of the well which he

had earlier climbed. He had believed the horn safe on its carrying strap. But when a handhold slipped, the strap slithered down from his shoulder and fell free, the horn with it.

Tense, Eric clung where he was, listening for the smash which would mark its landing. But he heard nothing. The thought of the horn's destruction made him so weak he was unable to move, his eyes watered, his stomach churned. What had he done in his carelessness?

All the many times in the past when Mother and Dad, Mrs. Steiner, Uncle Mac, yes, and Greg and Sara, too, had scolded him for being too fast, too impulsive, sang now in his spinning head. If the horn was broken what would happen? What could he say to Merlin and Huon? He had failed in his part of the quest.

Because he could not remain where he was, Eric hunted for the next hold on the wall. The spoon fastened to his belt clanged against the stone, but he did not care. The sky circle above him was dimming rapidly, cutting the light.

Eric descended slowly. If the impossible had happened and the horn had not been splintered to bits when it struck the ground, he had no wish to land on it himself. He clung tightly to the wall as his toes touched the bottom and then looked down and around eagerly.

But here those dim rays from the sky were gone. Eric went down on his knees and felt about him—then moved his hands faster, sifting sand, coarse gravel between his fingers, finding and discarding stones, until he had searched the whole floor of the well. Nowhere did he touch the leather strap or a battered curve of ivory and metal. The horn had completely disappeared!

Twice he searched the space, unable to believe that the horn was gone. Had the strap caught on some projection of the well wall, he would have brushed against it during his descent. So—

Eric's head was spinning, he was sure of nothing now. After one last sweep of his hands across the floor of the well, he headed back down the narrow passage to the sea cave.

The moist, salt-scented air of the cave puffed in his face, welcome after the ordeal in the nest. At the end of the short passage before he scrambled down to the beach, Eric lingered, peering out. The lapping of sea water against rocks was loud, but he was sure he heard another noise—a click—a grating.

Eric could make out the blot which was his boat, still out of the water as he had left it. He stood quite still, trying to keep the sound of his breathing to the faintest whisper. Although he could see nothing but the bulk of the boat, he believed there was another thing out there, a living creature with perhaps the power and will to attack—or damage—the boat on which his escape from the island depended.

Once again that sound—louder now as if who

or what was making it had no reason for concealment. Eric saw a dark shape flip into the air, outlined against the faint glimmer which marked the sea inlet.

That line ended in a monster claw, a claw which slowly opened and then snapped shut, as if its owner were flexing it before use. Then the clawed limb fell against the boat, and the light craft stirred in the sand, pushing toward the water. Eric knew he must act or the boat would be out in the pool beyond his reach.

His trust lay in the power of iron and he held the spoon as though it were a spear, the end of its bowl the point. Then he rushed that dark thing.

The spoon struck the side of the boat, bouncing off to a dark bulk which flinched and whipped away as if the tool were a branding iron. A jointed leg with its fearsome claw flashed up at Eric. The boy went down on one knee, holding the spoon to counter the blow, as he had held it to ward off the bird's beak. The claw struck forcibly, jamming Eric against the boat where his cheek rubbed raw on its scaled substance.

He cried out in pain, but there was no answer from the thing he fought. Eric could see only a black lump humping to the water. If it were able to escape into the sea, he could expect another attack.

Desperately Eric got to his feet, and holding the spoon over his head he ran forward, bringing the odd weapon down with all his might on the shambling creature. It slumped under the blow. He felt a stinging slash across his leg just below the knee. But he had won; the thing was no longer trying to reach water.

There were scrabbling sounds, as if many legs tried to lift a helpless weight of dying body. Then all was quiet.

Eric could not bring himself to touch the thing; he shrank from knowing what manner of creature he had fought. Sliding the spoon bowl under its bulk, he levered it into the pool. Then once again he felt the tangle of a strap about his foot, and eagerly he dug into the sand where the monster had lain, recovering the horn from where the dead thief had dropped it.

The Ring

The wood world awaited Sara now. As she sped toward the spider-web walls of the Castle of the Wood, strange new scents, smells which made her cat's nose twitch with excitement, arose from the ground under her paws and filled the air about her. She had never known before what it was really to be able to smell! Just as she had never known what it was to see. To her human eyes it had been dusk, a dimming of all color, a thickening and spreading of shadows. But now she could see into the heart of those shadows and so lost any fear of them.

But, though she was excited and pleased with her new body, her uneasiness returned in part as she neared the weirdly glowing spider webs. When she was still several feet away, she dropped the knife, planted both forefeet upon it for safety, and held her head as high as she could for a better look at the dead forest.

Sara shrank from touching the web. She had hoped to find a place where her cat's body might spring over the sticky band. But nowhere in sight was there any section where the outer trees were not coated from roots to lower branches with the stuff.

She must use the knife—but where? Some of the inborn caution of the animal whose shape she now wore came to her. She slipped through a growth of tall grass and crept on, the knife again gripped in her teeth.

Fearing unpleasant sentries, she dared not make too large and easily discovered a hole in the wall. So Sara hunted until she discovered a place where two mighty tree roots stood half out of the ground. Strands of web closed the gap between them, but it was a small gap. She crouched low and used her paws as well as her mouth to guide the knife. It was a clumsy business and took much longer than it would have done had she used hands and fingers. But the strands withered away and she had a free passage into the forest.

As she entered, flattening her body between the roots, Sara could see well enough. Very luckily the web did not extend beyond the first line of trees, and there were blobs of greenish-yellow light ahead.

The blobs were fungi growing on rotten wood. Sara's paw broke one, and the air was instantly filled with drifting motes of dust. She sneezed and then crowded her front paws against her nose. When she sneezed she had dropped the knife and that was dangerous. Quickly she picked it up again.

Any leaves which had fallen from the dead trees had long ago turned to dust, because the ground was bare black earth. She hated the slippery feel of it against her paws and, whenever she could, she walked along exposed roots or the trunks of fallen trees.

A human without a compass might have been lost in that maze where every tree copied its neighbor and the fungus lights confused the eye. But Sara's cat instinct took her without trouble toward the heart of this evil place.

She had not sighted any animal, bird, or insect. But she had a queer feeling that something lurked just beyond the limit of the eye, spying, waiting. And that Sara did not like at all.

Once she had to detour about a pool where the water was black and scummed. Bubbles rose slowly to the surface and broke. There Sara saw the first living thing, a pale, bleached lizard on a slimy rock, watching her with hard, glittering eyes.

At the other end of the pool Sara came upon faint traces of a path and she turned into it, eager to reach her goal. She had not forgotten caution, however, and it was with a cat's instant response to a danger signal that she halted at a faint sound. Was the lizard following?

Then she saw the enemy, not behind but to her right. A cluster of the fungus lights displayed its full horror. Sara tried to scream and the sound came from her furry throat as a hiss.

The thing ran along a tree trunk in a burst of speed she could not have bested and then halted. When it rested it was hardly distinguishable from one of the fungus lumps. Sara's claws dug into the ground as she flexed them. Warily she looked about, studying fungi which might not be fungi after all.

Her alarm grew. There were three, maybe four of the giant spiders drawing in about her. Had she not been alerted by the carelessness of the first, they might have surrounded her before she knew it. One she might attack, but not a whole ring of them.

A strand of thread floated lazily through the air. It drifted down, lay on Sara's furry back. There was another—and another! A web was being woven to enmesh her. But at that moment she feared the spiders themselves more than their handiwork and she planned desperately. She must allow herself to be trapped. Then, when they were sure of her, she would use the knife to escape.

It was very hard to do, waiting for the floating threads to coil about her. But Sara flattened her body to the ground, her paws drawn under her, the knife between them ready to be pushed forward. She shivered as the mat of threads caught on her ears, and hurriedly shut her eyes.

Once the net covered Sara's back and head, it fastened her tightly to the ground in a few seconds. She had to depend now on nose and ears to guide her. Legs raced across her imprisoned body and she shuddered as the spinners tested the silky bonds.

What if the spiders stung her now, left her paralyzed and helpless in the wrappings? She could smell their foulness, hear the faint rustle of their passing. They were circling, adding to the weight of the web.

Then a last tug on the smothering cover over her. The strong odor of the creatures faded. She strained to listen, to smell. If they left a sentry, there was no more than one. And one alone she could handle. Moving her paws against the ground, Sara pushed out the knife to touch her bonds.

There! Her right forefoot was free! Iron magic worked again. Sara arose from her crouch as the web broke and shriveled. She opened her eyes.

Facing her, standing erect on all its eight legs to challenge, was one of the spiders. It teetered back and forth and sprang. Sara struck with a front paw, knocked the creature to the ground, then swung the knife to touch it. She was not

125

sure Huon had been right—that iron was poisonous here. She could only hope so.

The spider pulled its legs under it, becoming a white-yellow lump. Sara took the haft of the knife in her mouth and jumped, pulling the blade across the insect's round body. The spider wriggled in sharp jerks, its legs flexed, and then drew up again. Sara prodded it with the knife, not wishing to touch it with her paw. When it did not move again, she laid the knife on the ground, keeping one paw on it, and with her tongue cleaned the remnants of the web from her fur.

Then, carrying the knife, she circled the dead spider and went on. But she was alert for another meeting with the creatures, watching every near fungus cluster with suspicion. It was very quiet in the dead wood, for there were no leaves to rustle, nothing but damp soil underfoot. Now that earth was giving away to flat stones which might have been old, old pavement.

The path dipped with banks of tree-grown earth rising on either side. Sara kept to its center, for in between those trees were more thick webs.

That sunken road brought her to a stream. This was no scummed pond but brown flowing water running in two ribbons about an island.

The outer rim of the island was a wall of stone so old and overgrown with dead vines and shaggy moss that it was hard to tell it from native rock. Once there might have been a bridge connecting it to the road, now there was only a series of water-washed stepping stones.

Sara prowled back and forth on the bank eying the stones doubtfully. Though she had not been told, she believed that the island was the center of the wood and held what she had come to find, but how to reach it was a problem. She could see unpleasant-looking water creatures swimming or moving back and forth on the stream bed, and she did not want to battle them. But could she leap from one wet stepping stone to the next without losing her footing?

She crouched, balancing the knife carefully in her mouth, and jumped to the first rock. It was slippery but she held fast. The second was flatter and better footing. There she sat, the knife under her forepaws, to study the third—for that had a rounded top and was green with slime. However, the fourth was another flat one. Could she leap to that from here? She crouched again, her hindquarters quivering, and tried.

Her hind feet splashed in the water as she scrabbled for a hold with her forepaws. There was a sharp pain in her tail and she heaved up and out. A clawed creature was pinching her tail tip, and Sara growled, swinging the creature against the knife so it tumbled off limply into the stream.

Wet fur made her cat body miserable, but she could not pause here to lick herself dry. For there was now another and longer jump to reach the top of the island wall. Clenching her teeth upon the knife, she made it. The wet hair on her spine rose in matted spikes, her ears folded to her skull, and her tail swung as she stood stiff-legged staring down at what that circle of ancient wall guarded.

The spiders of the forest were nasty creatures which she hated on sight, but here was worse —a toad three times the size of her present cat shape. It squatted motionless in the exact center of the open space, but its yellow eyes were fixed unblinkingly upon her and Sara feared it more than the spiders.

Her small body was shaking with more than the chill of the water. Those eyes—they were bigger—bigger—they were filling up the whole world! They were open places into which she might fall!

Sara blinked. It was dark, night had settled in. But those yellow toad eyes were bright enough to light up the island. The huge stretch of lips below them was opening—

She made herself as small a target as possible, the knife in her teeth. But the toad was so large, and the power of its eyes held her still. A black lash of tongue flickered out from between those huge lips, striving to whip her into the waiting mouth. But it touched the knife and snapped back.

The toad shivered, its bulk quivered, its mouth shut. Then out from between those lips fell a round, glowing bead which rolled to the foot of

the wall where Sara crouched. The bead was as clear as glass and at its core she saw a ring of dark metal.

The ring! In that moment she had to choose. She could not carry both ring and knife. If she took the talisman in her mouth she would have to leave behind her only weapon.

Sara moved quickly because she was afraid that if she waited she would not be able to do anything at all. She tossed the knife at the toad

129

and saw it land on the creature's broad back. The thing writhed and twisted, and then crumpled as might a bag from which air had escaped.

She sprang from the wall and snapped up the bead. It was hard to mouth but she held it.

"Kaaaw—" A black bird such as those which had followed her and the fox dived from the air, sounding its battle cry. Sara moved with terrified speed, making the passage of the stepping stones in bounds, returning to the shelter of the dead wood. She paused under that cover trying to plan, fearing to travel the spider-infested path without the knife.

She had dropped the bead between her paws and it was only at that moment she remembered that the ring itself was iron and so might be her protection. But first the glass shell about it must be broken.

Dropping it on a nearby rock did not crack the covering. She stood upon it with the full weight of her forepaws, but it only sank in the mold and did not break.

"Kaaaw—" One of the birds hopped along bare branches just above her and he was answered from the air. Sara took the bead in her mouth once more and ran at her best speed. As she went she bit at what she held, hoping her needle-sharp cat's teeth could crunch through.

With a leap she cleared the body of the spider guard where she had been trapped. Perhaps if she just kept running she could escape any harm.

But there was the beat of wings in the air, a quick stab of pain in one ear. Sara backed against a tree trunk where a mat of dead branches made cover to keep off the birds. She would have to break the bead or she would never get out of the wood, she was sure of that now.

With her nose and forepaws she wedged the globe against a half-buried stone and then, finding another such stone, she pushed it against the outer surface of the bead with all her strength, moving it slightly so that the globe was ground between the two rocks. She was losing hope in her plan when, with a small "pop," the bead was gone. Some dust glittered on the mold about the ring and that was all.

Sara mouthed the band, ready to run again. There was a scream from above. The birds were rising, leaving. Sure that she had a chance now, Sara ran, not realizing at first what was happening about her. For, as she sped among the trees, change spread with her.

Lumps of fungus dwindled, fell away. There was a cool wind rising, driving through the brittle branches, bringing with it a sweet cleanness. As she flashed about the pool where the lizard had lain, the water was no longer dull and scummed. It bubbled and sparkled, moved again by some long-choked spring.

When Sara reached the spot where she had crept beneath the web wall, she no longer faced the stretch of murky stuff. The web was now only bits of patches, for the wind was tearing at it, shredding it loose. So she ran easily out into the moonlight to climb the slope to where the fox waited.

At the top of the rise she paused to look back. All the dead trees were bending and twisting in the wind. Most of the web wall was gone. It was as if the strong blast of air was sweeping away all the evil which had hidden there, making it ready for life again. She saw a whirl of birds rise up against the moon. They wheeled as they flew toward her, uttering their hoarse calls.

Sara turned and ran at her best speed. Perhaps the wood was free of evil now, but it appeared that the black birds still had the power to hunt.

The Fox Gate

Before Greg was transformation indeed—change as great as Sara had seen in the wood. The village that had lain under the witch's spell came to life again. Its people, freed from their animal shapes, worked busily about their ruined homes. Two of those who had run as wolves now stood erect as lord and lady of the tower, to press upon Greg and his companions what shelter and food they had to offer. But when they had rested for a short space, Arthur's knight urged that they ride on, and now Greg was as impatient as he.

Though they pushed on into the gathering darkness, they did not lose their way, for, as the gloom thickened, there came a glow of light from the hilt of the great sword resting across the saddle before Greg, a light that was reflected and fed by a similar beam from the fork-spear. And this lighted their path as well as if a torch were being carried before them.

Where did the mountain road lead? Greg had entered it through Merlin's mirror and he had no idea of where it went beyond that point. He noticed that those who rode with him had their hands close to their sword hilts and that they kept careful watch of the heights on both sides of the road, as if fearing some ambush.

They came to the place where Greg had spent the night in his half cave. There it was necessary to dismount and pass one at a time, leading the horses down the broken slope. When they were once more on level ground, Greg was almost too tired to climb again into the saddle.

"Mount, young sir!" Arthur's knight urged him. "Time passes. Even now the east and the west may be facing the enemy. And how may Pendragon ride to battle without his blade? Mount —we must hurry!"

Painfully, Greg obeyed and rode on, nodding with weariness, not aware that the knight had taken his reins and was leading the horse he bestrode. But he roused quickly when the knight shouted an alarm.

The moon had risen and before them was drawn up a force, a silent barrier across the road. There were men—or things that looked like men—and these were flanked by monsters. Along their ranks, pointed at Arthur's men and at Greg himself, were blades of smoky red flame. At the back of this dark company was a shimmering silvery curtain—Merlin's mirror?

"Ho for Pendragon!" It was the knight who raised that cry as he drew his dwarf-forged blade. Those of his band echoed the cry and showed their own weapons.

Greg's horse, when the hold on the reins loosened, cantered on toward the line of the enemy. The boy heard the shouts of Arthur's men, the pound of hoofs on the roadway. His own horse, frightened, began to gallop. Points of dark fire gathered before Greg in a menacing wall. He held Excalibur tightly to his body with his left arm, while in his right hand he lifted the fork-spear. And the moonlight, pallid and weak though it was, centered on that, making it a banner of white flame. The dark wall wavered, moved before him. Greg cast the fork-spear, and the enemy's line curled back from its touch, while the horse galloped on toward the misty curtain.

Behind that, Greg saw a man mounted on one of the winged horses. He was a big man, with a golden beard and a helmet topped by a carven dragon with eyes of fire as red as the surcoat which covered the man's back and breast. Behind him was a great host of knights and archers under a banner that crackled in a high wind.

The bearded man faced Greg and held up his hand in a gesture of both entreaty and command. Somehow Greg found the strength he needed. Raising Excalibur in both hands, he hurled the sword up and out. End over end the giant blade went through the curtain. Then, as if drawn to a magnet, it flew to the outstretched hand of Arthur Pendragon. Three times the Warder of the East whirled the sword over his head as the banner behind him dipped in salute.

Then Greg's horse was at the edge of the mist, and Greg himself was engulfed in a swirl of fog. From afar he heard shouting, the clash of blade meeting blade, the singing of bowstrings. Then he rolled across grass and opened his eyes —to see above him, plain in the warm sun of afternoon, a fresh blaze cut upon a tree trunk.

Eric shrank back from the water into which the sea-thing had rolled. His first plan for spending the night in the cavern no longer pleased him. All he wanted was to return to shore, get away from the island as quickly as he could. He launched the boat, hoping to be free of the cave before the light utterly failed.

He kept the horn on his knees as he used the spoon paddle, determined not to lose it again. It took him much longer to edge through the narrow passage to the outer cave, for he feared ripping the skin covering of the craft on a rock, and he inched along until he could see the gray of evening reflected on the water ahead.

Against the lap of the waves, the sound of surf, Eric strained to hear any other noise. The monster

of the inner cave might not have been the only one of its kind abroad. Eric's worst fear was that something would rise from the depths to attack the boat.

It was more difficult to get out to sea than it had been to enter the cave originally. For then he had had the waves at his back and now he must head into them. Eric was so tired that every time he raised the spoon paddle his shoulders ached with the effort. But he made it at last, and gave a sigh of relief when he saw the island only a shadow on the sea, at his back instead of before him.

To Eric it seemed that that shadow reached in a black block from the island to the shore and that his path was covered by its gloom. The last red bands of the sunset were across the sky where it met the water, and in the air wheeled and called the sea birds.

They coasted on outstretched wings over the waves, skimming not far above his head. Surely they must be some of those that had perched upon the ledges to watch his battle with the monster. And now they followed him as if keeping watch. But for whom—for what?

Each slap of wave rocked the light boat. It would be so very easy for something to rise out of those waves, to turn the craft over. He must not think of that! His one bit of good fortune was that the shoreward wash of the waves carried the boat along, easing his paddling,

As the minutes passed and the beach drew nearer, Eric's confidence increased. So he was ill prepared for the trouble which did meet him.

The boat grounded gently and he jumped into the receding wash of the surf to draw it up. While the sea birds had seemed his enemies on the island, gathering to watch the attack of the giant bird, now they proved his friends. For, as Eric scrambled over the wet sand, the flock which had escorted him to land flew shrieking toward the dunes, uttering the same call they had given when he had leaped into the nest.

Eric spun around. The dunes made hills and valleys where the wind drove rippling sand. Coming out of several of those valleys were creatures no taller than he. They scuttled swiftly on webbed feet, moving to encircle him.

Their scaled skins gleamed wetly in the last glow of the sunset, the tangled mops of their green hair hung over their small eyes—which were fixed on Eric. If they kept on moving, they would push him back to the sea.

He held the horn and the spoon. The spoon had stood between him and the fury of the giant bird, had saved him in that battle in the cave with the unseen monster. Now it must clear a path through this mob of mermen. He twisted the sling of the horn through his belt, making very sure he could not lose it.

Then, holding the spoon before him, Eric moved straight ahead to meet the line of attack-

139

ers. A swift dip of his odd weapon into the sand,
a flip of grit into the faces of two of the creatures
sent them wiping frantically at their eyes as they
cried aloud in high, thin voices like the screams
of the sea birds. But others were closing in and
Eric swung the spoon. It jarred against one of
the mermen, who in turn stumbled against his
nearest fellow, tripping him up.

Eric sped through the gap so opened in their
line. He dodged into a space between two of the
dunes, only to face the rising slope of a third.
To climb the sandy hill at speed was, Eric
discovered, a difficult feat. At any moment he
expected to feel a webbed hand close about his
ankle and pull him down. But with aching ribs
and pounding heart he reached the top of the
rise, still ahead of his pursuers.

A green paw was grabbing for him, and behind
that leader the rest of the pack crowded close.
Their clamor shrilled in his ears, bewildering him.
Now they had ringed the foot of the dune, were
advancing from all sides. Eric did not see how he
could escape.

He chopped down at the first paw with the
spoon, made the leader tumble back. Then, because he could think of nothing else, he hurled
the spoon at the advance and brought the horn
to his lips—to blow with all the breath remaining
in his laboring lungs.

There was a thunderclap of sound. The green
men froze, then charged at him, yowling. But a

shimmering gray curtain was before him and
Eric, desperate, leaped through it.

On a windy hillside he faced Huon, who stood
brave in silver armor with a green surcoat, a
helmet on his head. Behind him were the knights
and archers from Caer Siddi, and over their heads
whipped in the wind the banner which had been
on the castle tower.

Though Eric believed he had securely fastened
the horn, it now left him, swinging up into the
air. Huon snatched it. With one hand he saluted

Eric, with the other he raised the horn to his lips. There was a second blast of sky-cracking sound and Eric was picked up by it, or by the wind, or by some strange force, and swept away.

Panting, he leaned against a tree. And before him, as tired and dirty as he was himself, Greg sprawled on the ground.

"Kaaaw—"

Sara leaped ahead, but a wing scraped across her tail. She kept her mouth clamped tight on the ring and fled at her best speed toward the marking of star and circle where the fox must be waiting. Now the black birds were attacking her as she had seen bluejays attack a cat, and she feared their sharp beaks and claws.

"Come! Come!" To human ears, that might only have been the bark of an excited fox, but to Sara it was a promise of help. The large red body of her woodsguide flashed down to circle her, snarling at the birds. But they were not to be driven off so easily.

Again Sara felt a sharp stab of pain as a claw racked her ear. She wanted to squawl her rage, but remembering the ring she held she kept her mouth shut and ran. Her pace was slowing, her throat was dry, her chest pained. There—there was the star-in-circle!

Now the fox was leaping into the air, battling the birds. Black feathers fluttered down. Her guide caught one body in his teeth and shook it limp. But the rest of them darted past him at Sara. She arose on her hind legs, striking out with unsheathed claws. Then she gave a last great spring and landed beside the basket table in the center of the star.

The fox barked and the birds swooped, still overhead.

"Use the ring! Change shape with the ring!"

Sara's mouth opened, the ring fell out upon the lid of the basket.

"Touch it and wish!" The fox bounded back and forth outside the circle.

Sara put up a footsore paw and laid it on the iron circlet.

"I want to be myself again," she meowed.

The fur on the back of her paw faded, the pads grew into fingers. Then, in a few more moments she was truly Sara again, outside as well as in, with a smarting scratch across her cheek, and so tired she could hardly move.

Once more the fox barked, but now she could no longer understand. He nodded his head vigorously toward the path in a way she could not mistake, and she got wearily to her feet. The ring! There it was on the lid of the basket. She picked it up and slipped it on her finger, doubling her fist about it for safekeeping. Then she hooked her arm through the handles of the basket and started after the fox.

The birds had drawn off the moment Sara had used the power of the ring. And, though she could still hear their harsh cries, they no longer flew to attack. But she was too tired to walk far.

However, the fox did not go with her on the woods path. Instead he slipped between two trees, giving reassuring barks and whines to urge her on.

They came to an opening in the woods where Sara could look through a frame of branches as one might look through a window. And she was not too surprised to see beyond the frame the room of the mirror where the tapestries still moved in the wind.

Merlin was there, facing her. He smiled and nodded, and held out his hand, palm up. Sara pulled the cold ring from her finger, glad to be free of it. She tossed it through the frame of branches and saw it fall into Merlin's grasp, his fingers close about it. Then the opening into the room of the mirror was gone and in its place was another stretch of woodland where Eric and Greg sat together under a tree, both of them looking very much as if they had been in a rough-and-tumble fight.

"Greg! Eric!" Sara broke through the bushes. She put down her basket and caught at her brothers to make sure that they were real and they were all truly together once more.

"Sara!" Both boys held her hands tightly. From behind came a sharp bark. The fox had followed her and now he trotted purposefully on, looking back over his shoulder in summons.

Sara was so used to obeying that gesture that

she freed her hands from her brothers' grasp and picked up the basket again.

"Come on."

They threaded a way among the trees until before them stood an arch of stone covered inches deep with green moss, with the carven mask of a fox set to crown its high point.

"The gate!" Eric ran forward. "We're able to go back—"

Sara turned to the fox and held out her hand. The big animal walked to her and just for a moment her fingers rested on his proud head. Then he barked impatiently and Greg pulled her on.

But there was no going through the gate. They could see no barrier but it was there, an invisible wall between them and their own world.

"What's the matter?" Eric's head was up, his face flushed, he was shouting aloud to the trees about them. "We got back your talismans, didn't we? Then open the gate! Right now!"

Sara looked at Greg and her lip trembled. She was almost as frightened now as she had been in that wicked wood among the spider hunters. Would they never be able to leave Avalon? It had been an exciting adventure, but she wanted it to end—right now!

"Open up!" Eric aimed his fist at the space between the stone pillars, only to have his hand rebound from an unseen surface.

Then, to one side there was a shimmering of

silver light. Sara caught at Greg's arm, Eric moved back. The tall column of silver broke into a mist of small, glittering sparks and in the midst stood Merlin.

On his robe the red lines twisted and climbed, blazing brighter than they ever had before, and the iron ring banded the forefinger of his raised hand.

Sara looked at the ring when she said, "We want to go home."

"Cold iron is master," he answered her. "You have left behind that which is not of Avalon and it binds you within this gate."

"The fork!" Greg cried out. "I lost it when we fought to reach King Arthur, back on the mountain road!"

"And the spoon," Eric broke in. "I dropped that on the dune where the sea people were."

"I threw the knife at the toad," Sara added. "Does that mean we have to go all the way back and find them again?"

"Iron, cold iron, answer iron—and your master!" Merlin turned the ring on his finger.

There was a tiny clatter and at his feet lay fork, spoon, and knife, their ordinary size again. Merlin beckoned with his ringed finger to Greg and the boy picked up the fork.

"Iron of spirit, iron of courage, making you the master of the dark and what may lie within it—the dark within, the dark without."

146

Then Merlin pointed to Eric, who took up the spoon.

"Iron of spirit, iron of courage, against fears within and fears without, waves and ripples of fear to be known no more."

It was Sara's turn, and as her fingers closed about the haft of the knife she heard Merlin's warm voice promising:

"Iron of spirit, iron of courage, mistress of fears whether they come gliding, crawling, or running on many legs!"

"Sir," Greg stood there, turning the fork about in his fingers, "what of the battle? Will King Arthur and Huon win?"

"Already they have driven back the enemy two leagues and ten. For this time Avalon still holds—and wins! Now"—he waved the ringed hand to the gate—"I conjure you, take your road and your cold iron with you. Also know this— Avalon gives thanks and Avalon cherishes her own. For you are now a part of her, which in time to come may be more to you than you can now guess. The gate is open. Go!"

Sara found herself running with Greg and Eric on either side. There was the mist curling about them and they were in the courtyard of the miniature castle once again.

"The door's gone!"

At Eric's cry the other two turned. All the stones they had picked out to make the passage were set back in place. And again the creeper wove a green veil there. Had they really gone through at all?

But in Greg's hand was a fork, Eric held a spoon, and Sara clutched the knife as well as the basket.

"Iron," began Greg and then corrected himself. "Steel magic."

A spider, very large and black, ran out of the vines, scuttled across the pavement by Sara's foot. She watched it go without withdrawing and said, half aloud, "Against fears whether they come gliding, crawling, or running on many legs." She looked again at the spider. Why, this creature was nothing at all compared to those she had fought in the webbed wood—nothing to be afraid of. It was just a bug! Iron of spirit, iron of courage. She wouldn't be afraid of the biggest spider in the garden from now on. Maybe Greg and Eric had not had time to try out their iron of courage yet, but she was sure it would work for them, too, and that they wouldn't need to carry spoon or fork to prove it.

"Hey!" Eric was already ahead of them, down the gravel bank leading to shore. "Hear that?" He kicked a stone into the lake defiantly— water was for drinking, washing—and for swimming. Water was only water.

A whistle—Uncle Mac's imperative signal.

"We're coming," Sara replied, clutching the basket tightly as she raced after her brothers.

About the Author

ANDRE NORTON was born in Cleveland and attended Western Reserve University. For many years, she worked as a children's librarian in the Cleveland Public Library. Miss Norton started her writing career as an editor of the literary page on her high school paper and published her first book before the age of twenty-one. She has written close to ninety books with millions of copies in print. In 1977, she received the Gandalf Award for her life's work in fantasy at the annual World Science Fiction Convention. FUR MAGIC, OCTAGON MAGIC, STAR KA'AT, and STAR KA'AT WORLD, by Andre Norton, are published in Archway Paperback editions.